致敬译界巨匠许渊冲先生

许渊冲译
诗经·风

BOOK OF POETRY
Book of Songs

译

中国出版集团
中译出版社

目录 Contents

周　南

002　关　雎
　　Cooing and Wooing

004　葛　覃
　　Home-going of the Bride

006　卷　耳
　　Mutual Longing

010　樛　木
　　Married Happiness

012　螽　斯
　　Blessed with Children

014　桃　夭
　　The Newly-wed

016　兔　罝
　　The Rabbit Catcher

018　芣　苢
　　Plantain Gathering

020　汉　广
　　A Woodcutter's Love

022　汝　坟
　　A Wife Waiting

024　麟之趾
　　The Good Unicorn

召　南

026　鹊　巢
　　The Magpie's Nest

028	采蘩	The Sacrifice
030	草虫	The Grasshoppers
032	采蘋	Sacrifice before Wedding
034	甘棠	The Duke of Shao
034	行露	I Accuse
036	羔羊	Officials in Lamb Furs
038	殷其雷	Why Not Return?
040	摽有梅	An Old Maid
042	小星	The Starlets
044	江有汜	A Merchant's Wife
046	野有死麕	A Deer Killer and a Jadelike Maiden
046	何彼襛矣	The Princess' Wedding
048	驺虞	A Hunter

邶 风

050 柏 舟
Depression

054 绿 衣
My Green Robe

056 燕 燕
A Farewell Song

058 日 月
Sun And Moon

060 终 风
The Violent Wind

062 击 鼓
Complaint of a Soldier

066 凯 风
Our Mother

068 雄 雉
My Man in Service

070 匏有苦叶
Waiting for Her Fiance

072 谷 风
A Rejected Wife

076 式 微
Toilers

078 旄 丘
Refugees

080 简 兮
A Dancer

082	泉　水 Fair Spring	
086	北　门 A Petty Official	
088	北　风 The Hard Pressed	
090	静　女 A Shepherdess	
092	新　台 The New Tower	
094	二子乘舟 Two Sons in a Boat	

鄘　风

096	柏　舟 A Cypress Boat	
098	墙有茨 Scandals	
100	君子偕老 Duchess Xuan Jiang of Wei	
102	桑　中 Trysts	
104	鹑之奔奔 Misfortune	
106	定之方中 Duke Wen of Wei	
108	蝃　蝀 Elopement	

110	相 鼠 The Rat	
112	干 旄 Betrothal Gifts	
114	载 驰 Patriotic Baroness Mu of Xu	

卫 风

118	淇 奥 Duke Wu of Wei	
120	考 槃 A Happy Hermit	
122	硕 人 The Duke's Bride	
126	氓 A Faithless Man	
132	竹 竿 A Lovesick Fisherman	
134	芄 兰 A Widow in Love	
136	河 广 The River Wide	
136	伯 兮 My Lord	
140	有 狐 A Lonely Husband	
140	木 瓜 Gifts	

王 风

144	黍 离 The Ruined Capital	
146	君子于役 My Man Is Away	
148	君子阳阳 What Joy	
150	扬之水 In Garrison	
152	中谷有蓷 Grief of a Deserted Wife	
154	兔爰 Past and Present	
156	葛藟 A Refugee	
158	采 葛 One Day When I See Her Not	
160	大 车 To Her Captive Lord	
162	丘中有麻 To Her Lover	

郑 风

164	缁 衣 A Good Wife	
166	将仲子 Cadet My Dear	

168	叔于田	The Young Cadet
170	大叔于田	Hunting
172	清　人	Qing Warriors
174	羔　裘	Officer in Lamb's Fur
176	遵大路	Leave Me Not
178	女曰鸡鸣	A Hunter's Domestic Life
180	有女同车	Lady Jiang
180	山有扶苏	A Joke
182	萚　兮	Sing Together
182	狡　童	A Handsome Guy
184	褰　裳	Lift up Your Robe
186	丰	Lost Opportunity
188	东门之墠	A Lover's Monologue
188	风　雨	Wind and Rain

190	子 衿	To a Scholar
192	扬之水	Believe Me
192	出其东门	My Lover in White
194	野有蔓草	The Creeping Grass
196	溱 洧	Riverside Rendezvous

齐 风

200	鸡 鸣	A Courtier and His Wife
202	还	Two Hunters
204	著	The Bridegroom
204	东方之日	Nocturnal Tryst
206	东方未明	A Tryst before Dawn
208	南 山	Incest
210	甫 田	Missing Her Son
212	卢 令	Hunter and Hounds

214	敝　笱
	Duchess Wen Jiang of Qi
216	载　驱
	Duke of Qi and Duchess of Lu
218	猗　嗟
	The Archer Duke

魏　风

220	葛　屦
	A Well-Drest Lady and Her Maid
222	汾沮洳
	A Scholar Unknown
224	园有桃
	A Scholar Misunderstood
226	陟　岵
	A Homesick Soldier
228	十亩之间
	Gathering Mulberry
228	伐　檀
	The Woodcutter's Song
232	硕　鼠
	Large Rat

唐　风

236	蟋　蟀
	The Cricket
238	山有枢
	Why Not Enjoy?

240	扬之水	Our Prince
242	椒　聊	The Pepper Plant
244	绸　缪	A Wedding Song
246	杕　杜	A Wanderer
250	羔　裘	An Unkind Lord in Lamb's Fur
250	鸨　羽	The Peasants' Complaint
252	无　衣	To His Deceased Wife
254	有杕之杜	The Russet Pear Tree
254	葛　生	An Elegy
256	采　苓	Rumor

秦　风

260	车　邻	Lord Zhong of Qin
262	驷　驖	Winter Hunting
264	小　戎	A Lord on Expedition

268	蒹　葭 Where Is She?
270	终　南 Duke Xiang of Qin
272	黄　鸟 Burial of Three Worthies
274	晨　风 The Forgotten
276	无　衣 Comradeship
278	渭　阳 Farewell to Duke Wen of Jin
280	权　舆 Not As Before

陈　风

282	宛　丘 A Religious Dancer
284	东门之枌 Secular Dancers
284	衡　门 Contentment
286	东门之池 To a Weaving Maiden
288	东门之杨 A Date
288	墓　门 The Evil-Doing Usurper

290	防有鹊巢	Riverside Magpies
292	月　出	The Moon
294	株　林	The Duke's Mistress
294	泽　陂	A Bewitching Lady

桧　风

298	羔　裘	The Last Lord of Kuai
300	素　冠	The Mourning Wife
300	隰有苌楚	The Unconscious Tree
304	匪　风	Nostalgia

曹　风

306	蜉　蝣	The Ephemera
308	候　人	Poor Attendants
310	鸤　鸠	An Ideal Ruler
312	下　泉	The Canal

豳 风

316	七 月 Life of Peasants
326	鸱 鸮 A Mother Bird
328	东 山 Coming Back From the Eastern Hills
334	破 斧 With Broken Axe
336	伐 柯 An Axe-handle
336	九 罭 The Duke's Return
338	狼 跋 Like an Old Wolf

风
·
·
·

Book of Songs

周　南

关　雎

关关^①雎鸠^②，
在河之洲。
窈窕淑女，
君子好逑。

参差荇菜，
左右流^③之。
窈窕淑女，
寤寐求之。

求之不得，
寤寐思服。
悠哉悠哉，
辗转反侧。

关关和唱的鱼鹰，
在河中小洲之上。
美丽善良的姑娘啊，
是君子追求的对象。

长长短短的荇菜，
左左右右地采摘。
美丽善良的姑娘啊，
想她想到梦里来。

追求不到那姑娘，
却是醒也思梦也想。
想念她啊想念她，
翻来覆去到天亮。

---

① 关关：雌雄两鸟的和鸣声。
② 雎鸠：一种水鸟，相传这种鸟雌雄间的爱情很专一。
③ 流：顺着水流之势而择取。

Songs Collected South of the Capital, Modern Shaanxi and Henan

Cooing and Wooing[1]

By riverside a pair
Of turtledoves are cooing;
There is a maiden fair
whom a young man is wooing.

Water flows left and right
Of cresses here and there;
The youth yearns day and night
For the maiden so fair.

His yearning grows so strong,
He cannot fall asleep,
But tosses all night long,
So deep in love, so deep!

---

[1] The young man made acquaintance with the maiden in spring when turtledoves were cooing (Stanza 1), wooed her in summer when cress floated on water (Stanza 2) and yearned for her until they were engaged in autumn when cress was gathered (Stanza 4) and married in winter when cresses were cooked (Stanza 5).

参差荇菜，　　　　　　　　长长短短的荇菜，
左右采之。　　　　　　　　左左右右地采摘。
窈窕淑女，　　　　　　　　美丽善良的姑娘啊，
琴瑟友之。　　　　　　　　弹琴鼓瑟把她爱。

参差荇菜，　　　　　　　　长长短短的荇菜，
左右芼^①之。　　　　　　　　左左右右地采摘。
窈窕淑女，　　　　　　　　美丽善良的姑娘啊，
钟鼓乐之。　　　　　　　　敲钟打鼓取悦她。

葛 覃

葛^②之覃^③兮，　　　　　　　　葛藤长长，
施^④于中谷，　　　　　　　　缠蔓山沟里，
维叶萋萋。　　　　　　　　叶子密层层。
黄鸟于飞，　　　　　　　　轻飞是黄莺，
集于灌木，　　　　　　　　落入灌木丛，
其鸣喈喈。　　　　　　　　叽叽叫不停。

葛之覃兮，　　　　　　　　葛藤长长，
施于中谷，　　　　　　　　缠蔓山沟里，
维叶莫莫。　　　　　　　　叶子密层层。

---

① 芼：采摘。
② 葛：一种多年生蔓草，可以用来织布。
③ 覃：延长。
④ 施：蔓延。

Now gather left and right
Cress long or short and tender!
O lute, play music light
For the fiancée so slender!

Feast friends at left and right
On cresses cooked tender!
O bells and drums, delight
The bride so sweet and slender!

Home-going of the Bride[①]

The vines outspread and trail
In the midst of the vale.
Their leaves grow lush and sprout;
Yellow birds fly about
And perch on leafy trees.
O how their twitters please!

The vines outspread and trail
In the midst of the vale.
Their leaves grow lush on soil,

---

① Going back to her parents' home was an important event for a bride after her wedding.

是刈①是濩②,　　　　　　割煮忙又忙,
为絺③为绤④,　　　　　　织成粗布和细布,
服之无斁⑤。　　　　　　穿在身上多舒畅。
言告师氏,　　　　　　　向我保姆告个假,
言告言归。　　　　　　　我要回娘家。
薄污⑥我私⑦,　　　　　　洗了我的内衣,
薄浣⑧我衣。　　　　　　洗了我的外褂。
害浣害⑨否?　　　　　　还要洗啥,不要洗啥?
归宁⑩父母。　　　　　　就要回家见爹妈。

卷 耳⑪

采采卷耳,　　　　　　　采啊采啊采卷耳,
不盈顷筐。　　　　　　　总是不满小浅筐。
嗟我怀人,　　　　　　　一心想着远行人,
置⑫彼周行⑬。　　　　　　把筐放在大路旁。

---

① 刈:割。
② 濩:煮。
③ 絺(chī):细葛布。
④ 绤(xì):粗葛布。
⑤ 斁(yì):厌恶。
⑥ 污:洗涤。
⑦ 私:内衣。
⑧ 浣:洗涤。
⑨ 害:何,哪一个。
⑩ 归宁:回家问候父母。
⑪ 卷耳:一种植物,嫩苗可以吃,也可以药用。
⑫ 置:放。
⑬ 周行:大道。

So good to cut and boil
And make cloth coarse or fine.
Who wears it likes the vine.
I tell Mother-in-law
Soon I will homeward go.
I'll wash my undershirt
And rinse my outerskirt.
My dress cleaned, I'll appear
Before my parents dear.

Mutual Longing[①]

Wife: "I gather the mouse-ear
With a basket to fill.
I miss my husband dear
And leave it empty still."

---

① A wife was longing for the return of her husband while he was longing for her on his homeward way.

陟①彼崔嵬②，　　　　　　登上石山高又险，
我马虺隤③。　　　　　　　我的马儿腿发软。
我姑酌彼金罍，　　　　　　先把酒壶来倒满，
维以不永怀。　　　　　　　好让心儿静又安。

陟彼高冈，　　　　　　　　攀上山梁陡又狭，
我马玄黄④。　　　　　　　我的马儿眼发花。
我姑酌彼兕觥，　　　　　　先把酒杯来倒满，
维以不永伤。　　　　　　　好让心儿免悲伤。

陟彼砠⑤矣，　　　　　　　艰难登上土石山，
我马瘏⑥矣，　　　　　　　我的马儿要累倒，
我仆痡⑦矣，　　　　　　　我的仆人要累病，
云何吁矣！　　　　　　　　这种忧伤何时了！

---

① 陟：登。
② 崔嵬：高山。
③ 虺隤（huī tuí）：疲惫难行。
④ 玄黄：指因病而变色，眼花。
⑤ 砠：有土的石山。
⑥ 瘏（tú）：劳累过度。
⑦ 痡（fū）：疲病。

Man: "The hill I'm climbing up
Has tried and tired my horse.
I'll drink my golden cup
So as to gather force.

"The height I'm climbing up
Has dizzied my horse in strife.
I drink my rhino cup
Lest I'd think of my wife.

"I climb the rocky hill;
My wornout horse won't go.
My servant's very ill.
O how great is my woe!"

樛 木①

南有樛木,　　　　　　　　南山有棵弯弯树,
葛藟②累之。　　　　　　　野葛都来攀缘它。
乐只君子,　　　　　　　　这样快乐的君子,
福履③绥之!　　　　　　　上天降福赐给他!

南有樛木,　　　　　　　　南山有棵弯弯树,
葛藟荒④之。　　　　　　　野葛都来遮掩它。
乐只君子,　　　　　　　　这样快乐的君子,
福履将之!　　　　　　　　上天降福保佑他!

南有樛木,　　　　　　　　南山有棵弯弯树,
葛藟萦之。　　　　　　　　野葛都来缠绕它。
乐只君子,　　　　　　　　这样快乐的君子,
福履成之!　　　　　　　　上天降福成全他!

① 樛木:树木向下弯曲。
② 葛藟:野葛。
③ 福履:福禄。
④ 荒:掩盖。

Married Happiness[1]

Up crooked Southern trees
Are climbing creepers' vines;
On lords whom their wives please,
Quiet happiness shines.

The crooked Southern trees
Are covered by grapevines;
On lords whom their wives please,
Greater happiness shines.

Round crooked Southern trees
Are twining creepers' vines;
On lords whom their wives please,
Perfect happiness shines.

---

[1] A wife was to her lord as the vine was to the tree.

螽　斯[①]

螽斯羽[②]，　　　　　　　螽儿的翅膀，
诜诜[③]兮。　　　　　　　密密地排。
宜尔子孙，　　　　　　　你子孙多啊，
振振[④]兮。　　　　　　　兴旺无法量。

螽斯羽，　　　　　　　　螽儿的翅膀，
薨薨[⑤]兮。　　　　　　　翁翁地响。
宜尔子孙，　　　　　　　你子孙多啊，
绳绳兮。　　　　　　　　绵延无限长。

螽斯羽，　　　　　　　　螽儿的翅膀，
揖揖[⑥]兮。　　　　　　　群集会聚。
宜尔子孙，　　　　　　　你子孙多啊，
蛰蛰[⑦]兮。　　　　　　　团聚真欢畅。

① 螽：蝗虫的一种。斯，的。
② 羽：翅膀。
③ 诜诜（shēn shēn）：和顺的声音。
④ 振振（zhēn zhēn）：众多的样子。
⑤ 薨薨：繁多的样子。
⑥ 揖揖：聚集。
⑦ 蛰蛰（zhí zhí）：集和。

Blessed with Children[①]

Insects in flight,
Well you appear.
It is all right
To teem with children dear.

Insects in flight,
How sound your wings!
It is all right
To have children in strings.

Insects in flight,
You feel so warm.
It is all right
To have children in swarm.

[①] The poet wished the family to be blessed with as many children as a swarm of insects.

桃 夭

桃之夭夭[①],　　　　　　　桃树茂盛枝杈嫩,
灼灼[②]其华。　　　　　　　开的花儿红又粉。
之子[③]于归[④],　　　　　　这个姑娘要出嫁,
宜其室家。　　　　　　　　和顺对待夫家人。

桃之夭夭,　　　　　　　　桃树茂盛枝杈嫩,
有蕡[⑤]其实。　　　　　　　结的果儿红又润。
之子于归,　　　　　　　　这个姑娘要出嫁,
宜其家室。　　　　　　　　和顺对待夫家人。

桃之夭夭,　　　　　　　　桃树茂盛枝杈嫩,
其叶蓁蓁[⑥]。　　　　　　　长的叶儿绿又肥。
之子于归,　　　　　　　　这个姑娘要出嫁,
宜其家人。　　　　　　　　和顺对待夫家人。

① 夭夭:树因为年轻而长得茂盛。
② 灼灼:红红的。
③ 之子:这个姑娘。
④ 于归:出嫁。
⑤ 蕡(fén):大。
⑥ 蓁蓁:繁盛的样子。

The Newly-wed[①]

The peach tree beams so red;
How brilliant are its flowers!
The maiden's getting wed,
Good for the nuptial bowers.

The peach tree beams so red;
How plentiful its fruit!
The maiden's getting wed;
She's the family's root.

The peach tree beams so red;
Its leaves are lush and green.
The maiden's getting wed;
On household she'll be keen.

---

① Under the Zhou dynasty (1121—255 B. C.) young people were married in spring when the peach tree was in flower. This was the first nuptial song in Chinese history, in which the beauty of the bride was compared to that of peach blossoms.

兔 罝[1]

肃肃兔罝,	严严实实结兔网,
椓[2]之丁丁。	木桩敲得当当响。
赳赳武夫,	赳赳武夫真勇猛,
公侯干城[3]。	公侯把他做屏障。
肃肃兔罝,	严严实实结兔网,
施于中逵[4]。	放在大路正中央。
赳赳武夫,	赳赳武夫真勇猛,
公侯好仇[5]。	公侯把他做伴当。
肃肃兔罝,	严严实实结兔网,
施于中林。	放在树林正中央。
赳赳武夫,	赳赳武夫真勇猛,
公侯腹心。	公侯心腹守四方。

[1] 罝：网。
[2] 椓：敲打。
[3] 干城：城墙，屏障。
[4] 中逵：大路。
[5] 仇：伴当，搭档。

The Rabbit Catcher[1]

Well set are rabbit nets;
On the pegs go the blows.
The warrior our lord gets
Protects him from the foes.

Well set are rabbit nets,
Placed where crossroads appear.
The warrior our lord gets
Will be his good compeer.

Well set are rabbit nets,
Amid the forest spread.
The warrior our lord gets
Serves him with heart and head.

[1] This was a song in praise of a rabbit catcher, fit to be a warrior and compeer of the lord. It set forth the influence of the lord as so powerful and beneficial that individuals of the lowest rank might be made fit to occupy the highest positions.

芣 苢[①]

采采芣苢，	鲜亮亮的车前子呀，
薄言采之。	快呀快呀采摘它。
采采芣苢，	鲜亮亮的车前子呀，
薄言有之。	快呀快呀收起它。

采采芣苢，	鲜亮亮的车前子呀，
薄言掇之。	快呀快呀拾取它。
采采芣苢，	鲜亮亮的车前子呀，
薄言捋之。	快呀快呀捋取它。

采采芣苢，	鲜亮亮的车前子呀，
薄言袺[②]之。	翻过衣襟装起它。
采采芣苢，	鲜亮亮的车前子呀，
薄言襭[③]之。	提起衣襟兜满它。

---

① 芣苢（fú yǐ）：车前子，叶可食用，实可药用。
② 袺：手执衣襟以承物。
③ 襭：翻动衣襟以承物。

Plantain Gathering[1]

We gather plantain seed.
Let's gather it with speed!
We gather plantain ears.
Let's gather them with cheers!

We gather plantain seed.
Let's rub it out with speed!
We gather plantain ears.
Pull by handfuls with cheers!

We gather plantain seed.
Let's fill our skirts with speed!
We gather plantain ears.
Belt up full skirts with cheers!

---

[1] This song was sung by women while gathering plantain seed which was thought to be favorable to child-bearing and difficult labors.

汉 广

南有乔木①,	南方有棵高高树,
不可休思。	树下少荫不可休。
汉有游女,	汉江有个好游女,
不可求思。	枉费心思不可求。
汉之广矣,	汉江之水广又宽,
不可泳思。	游过好比登天难。
江之永矣,	好似汉江长又长,
不可方②思。	航行不能用小舫。
翘翘错薪,	丛丛柴草长得高,
言刈其楚。	割柴最好割荆条。
之子于归,	有个姑娘要出嫁,
言秣③其马。	先把马儿来喂饱。
汉之广矣,	汉江之水广又宽,
不可泳思。	游过好比登天难。
江之永矣,	好似汉江长又长,
不可方思。	航行不能用小舫。

① 乔木:高大的树木。
② 方:舫,小舟。
③ 秣:用草喂马。

A Woodcutter's Love[①]

The tallest Southern tree
Affords no shade for me.
The maiden on the stream
Can but be found in dream.
For me the stream's too wide
To reach the other side
As River Han's too long
To cross its current strong.

Of the trees in the wood
I'll only cut the good.
If she should marry me,
Her stable-man I'd be.
For me the stream's too wide
To reach the other side
As River Han's too long
To cross its current strong.

---

① The legend said that there was a Goddess on the River Han. Here the woodcutter compared the maiden he loved to the inaccessible Goddess.

翘翘错薪，	丛丛柴草长得高，
言刈其蒌①。	割柴最好割芦蒿。
之子于归，	有个姑娘要出嫁，
言秣其驹。	先把马驹来喂饱。
汉之广矣，	汉江之水广又宽，
不可泳思。	游过好比登天难。
江之永矣，	好似汉江长又长，
不可方思。	航行不能用小舫。

汝 坟②

遵③彼汝坟，	沿着汝水走堤岸，
伐其条枚④。	先砍树枝再砍干。
未见君子，	没有见到我君子，
惄⑤如调⑥饥。	忧似忍饥在晨朝。

遵彼汝坟，	沿着汝水走堤岸，
伐其条肄。	砍那新生树枝条。
既见君子，	已经见到我君子，
不我遐弃。	幸未曾把我远抛。

---

① 蒌：多长在水边的一种植物，叶嫩时可食，老时可为薪。
② 坟：河堤。
③ 遵：沿着。
④ 枚：树干。
⑤ 惄（nì）：忧思。
⑥ 调：整个早晨。

Of the trees here and there
I'll only cut the fair.
If she should marry me,
Her stable-boy I'd be.
For me the stream's too wide
To reach the other side
As River Han's too long
To cross its current strong.

A Wife Waiting[①]

Along the raised bank green
I cut down twigs and wait.
My lord cannot be seen;
I feel a hunger great.

Along the raised bank green
I cut fresh sprigs and spray.
My lord can now be seen,
But soon he'll go away.

---

① A wife tried to dissuade her lord from leaving her again by cooking for him a red-tailed fish to show the unfed flame of her heart.

鲂鱼赪①尾，　　　　　　　鲂鱼尾红因疲劳，
王室如燬②。　　　　　　　王朝多难如火烧。
虽则如燬，　　　　　　　　虽然多难如火烧，
父母孔迩。　　　　　　　　父母供奉莫忘掉。

麟之趾

麟之趾，　　　　　　　　　麟的脚趾不踏生物，
振振③公子。　　　　　　　好比仁厚的公子。
于嗟麟兮！　　　　　　　　值得赞美的麟啊！

麟之定，　　　　　　　　　麟的额头不顶生灵，
振振公姓。　　　　　　　　好比仁厚的公孙。
于嗟麟兮！　　　　　　　　值得赞美的麟啊！

麟之角，　　　　　　　　　麟的头角不触万物，
振振公族。　　　　　　　　好比仁厚的公族。
于嗟麟兮！　　　　　　　　值得赞美的麟啊！

① 赪（chēng）：赤色。
② 燬：火烧。
③ 振振：仁厚的样子。

"I'll leave your red-tailed fish:
The kingdom is on fire."
"If you leave as you wish,
Who'll take care of your sire?"

The Good Unicorn[1]

The unicorn will use its hoofs to tread on none
Just like our Prince's noble son.
Ah! they are one.

The unicorn will knock its head against none
Just like our Prince's grandson.
Ah! they are one.

The unicorn will fight with its corn against none
Just like our Prince's great-grand-son.
Ah! they are one.

---

[1] The unicorn was a fabulous animal, the symbol of all goodness and benevolence, having the body of a deer, the tail of an ox, the hoofs of a horse, one horn in the middle of the forehead. Its hoofs were mentioned because it did not tread on any living thing, not even on live grass; its head because it did not butt with it; and its horn because the end of it was covered with flesh, to show that the creature, while able for war, would have peace. This song celebrated the goodness of the offspring of King Wen (1184—1134 B. C.), founder of the Zhou dynasty.

召　南

鹊　巢

维鹊有巢,
维鸠①居之。
之子于归,
百两御之。

喜鹊树上有个巢,
斑鸠飞来居住它。
这个姑娘要出嫁,
百辆车子迎接她。

维鹊有巢,
维鸠方②之。
之子于归,
百两将之。

喜鹊树上有个巢,
斑鸠飞来占住它。
这个姑娘要出嫁,
百辆车子恭送她。

维鹊有巢,
维鸠盈之。
之子于归,
百两成之。

喜鹊树上有个巢,
斑鸠飞来占满它。
这个姑娘要出嫁,
百辆车子成就她。

① 鸠:斑鸠,占住其他鸟巢的一种鸟。
② 方:占有。

Songs Collected South of Zhao, Modern Henan

The Magpie's Nest[1]

The magpie builds a nest,
Where comes the dove in spring.
The bride comes fully-drest,
Welcomed by cabs in string.

The magpie builds a nest,
Where dwells the dove in spring.
The bride comes fully-drest,
Escort'd by cabs in string.

The magpie builds a nest,
Where lives the dove in spring.
The bride comes fully-drest,
Celebrated by cabs in string.

---

[1] The newly-wed were compared to magpie and dove or myna. The bride came escorted and welcomed by cabs and the wedding was celebrated by cabs.

采 蘩

于以采蘩?	什么地方采白蒿?
于沼于沚。	水中小洲和湖沼。
于以用之?	什么地方能用到?
公侯之事。	公侯祭祀他祖考。
于以采蘩?	什么地方采白蒿?
于涧之中。	幽深山涧能找到。
于以用之?	什么地方能用到?
公侯之宫。	公侯祭祀他祖庙。
被①之僮僮②,	首饰佩戴得整齐,
夙夜在公。	早晚参加祭祀礼。
被之祁祁③,	首饰佩戴得华丽,
薄言还归。	祭祀完毕回家去。

① 被 (bì): 首饰。
② 僮僮: 盛大。
③ 祁祁: 繁盛的样子。

The Sacrifice[1]

Gather southernwood white
By the pools here and there.
Employ it in the rite
In our prince's affair.

Gather southernwood white
In the vale by the stream.
Employ it in the rite
Under the temple's beam.

Wearing black, gloosy hair,
We're busy all the day.
With disheveled hair
At dusk we go away.

[1] This song narrates the industry of the chambermaids assisting the prince in sacrificing.

草　虫

喓喓①草虫，
趯趯②阜螽③。
未见君子，
忧心忡忡④。
亦既见止，
亦既觏⑤止，
我心则降。

蟋蟀喓喓叫，
蚱蜢蹦蹦跳。
没有见君子，
心绪乱如搅。
如果已经相见了，
如果已经相聚了，
我心平静不焦躁。

陟彼南山，
言采其蕨。
未见君子，
忧心惙惙⑥。
亦既见止，
亦既觏止，
我心则说。

登到南山上，
要去采蕨菜。
没有见君子，
心里愁得慌。
如果已经相见了，
如果已经相聚了，
我心欢乐多舒畅。

陟彼南山，
言采其薇。
未见君子，
我心伤悲。

登到南山上，
要去采薇菜。
没有见君子，
心里悲得凄。

① 喓喓：虫叫的声音。
② 趯趯（tì tì）：跳跃。
③ 阜螽：蚱蜢。
④ 忡忡：心跳。
⑤ 觏：相会。
⑥ 惙惙（chuò chuò）：惶惑。

The Grasshoppers[1]

Hear grassland insects sing
And see grasshoppers spring!
When my lord is not seen,
I feel a sorrow keen.
When I see him downhill
And meet him by the rill,
My heart would then be still.

I go up southern hill;
Of ferns I get my fill.
When my lord is not seen,
I feel a grief more keen.
When I see him downhill
And meet him by the rill,
My heart with joy would thrill.

I go up southern hill;
Of herbs I get my fill.
When my lord is not seen,
I feel a grief most keen.

---

[1] A wife was longing for her lord from autumn when grasshoppers sang, to spring when fern was gathered, and to summer when herb was gathered.

亦既见止，　　　　　　　　如果已经相见了，
亦既觏止，　　　　　　　　如果已经相聚了，
我心则夷①。　　　　　　　我心安详多欣喜。

采 蘋

于以采蘋？　　　　　　　　什么地方采蘋草？
南涧之滨。　　　　　　　　南山溪水边。
于以采藻？　　　　　　　　什么地方采浮藻？
于彼行潦②。　　　　　　　沟水积水边。

于以盛之？　　　　　　　　什么东西装盛它？
维筐及筥③。　　　　　　　圆篓和方筐。
于以湘④之？　　　　　　　什么器具蒸煮它？
维锜⑤及釜。　　　　　　　三脚没脚釜。

于以奠之？　　　　　　　　什么地方祭献它？
宗室牖⑥下。　　　　　　　宗室窗子下。
谁其尸⑦之？　　　　　　　什么人来主祭啊？
有齐⑧季女。　　　　　　　斋戒小女娃。

---

① 夷：平。
② 行潦：流动的水沟，积水。
③ 筥（jǔ）：圆竹器。
④ 湘：烹煮。
⑤ 锜（qí）：三足的釜。
⑥ 牖：窗子。
⑦ 尸：主持。古代祭祀时被当作神的人。
⑧ 齐：通"斋"，斋戒。

When I see him downhill
And meet him by the rill,
My heart would be serene.

Sacrifice before Wedding[①]

Where to gather duckweed?
In the brook by south hill.
Where to gather pondweed?
Between the brook and rill.

Where to put what we've found?
In baskets square or round.
Where to boil what we can?
In the tripod or pan.

Where to put offerings?
In the temple's both wings.
Who offers sacrifice?
The bride-to-be so nice.

---

① According to ancient custom, the bride-to-be should gather duckweed and offer it as sacrifice in the temple three months before her wedding.

甘 棠

蔽芾①甘棠，　　　　　　　茂盛的棠梨树，
勿翦勿伐，　　　　　　　　不剪不砍它，
召伯所茇②。　　　　　　　召伯曾停留在树下。

蔽芾甘棠，　　　　　　　　茂盛的棠梨树，
勿翦勿败，　　　　　　　　不剪不折它，
召伯所憩。　　　　　　　　召伯曾歇息在树下。

蔽芾甘棠，　　　　　　　　茂盛的棠梨树，
勿翦勿拜，　　　　　　　　不剪不弯它，
召伯所说③。　　　　　　　召伯曾住宿在树下。

行 露

厌浥④行露。　　　　　　　道上的露水湿漉漉，
岂不夙夜，　　　　　　　　难道清早不走路，
谓行多露？　　　　　　　　就怕道上的湿露？

---

① 蔽芾：茂盛。
② 茇（bá）：草舍，这里指在树下休息。
③ 说：通"税"，住宿，休息。
④ 厌浥：被露水沾湿。

The Duke of Shao[①]

O leafy tree of pear!
Don't clip or make it bare,
For once our Duke lodged there.

O leafy tree of pear!
Don't break its branches bare,
For once our Duke rested there.

O leafy tree of pear!
Don't bend its branches bare,
For once our Duke halted there.

I Accuse[②]

The path with dew is wet;
Before dawn off I set;
I fear nor dew nor threat.

---

① The Duke of Shao was a principal adherent of King Wen. The love of the people for the memory of the Duke of Shao made them love the tree beneath which he had rested.
② A young woman resisted an attempt to force her to marry a married man and she argued her cause though put in jail and brought to the judge's hall.

谁谓雀无角，　　　　　　谁说雀儿没有角，
何以穿我屋？　　　　　　怎么会啄穿我的屋？
谁谓女无家，　　　　　　谁说你未娶已成家，
何以速我狱？　　　　　　怎么要送我去监狱？
虽速我狱，　　　　　　　就是送我去监狱，
室家①不足。　　　　　　强迫结婚无道理。

谁谓鼠无牙，　　　　　　谁说老鼠没有牙，
何以穿我墉？　　　　　　怎么会打通我的墙？
谁谓女无家，　　　　　　谁说你未娶已成家，
何以速我讼？　　　　　　怎么逼我上公堂？
虽速我讼，　　　　　　　就算逼我上公堂，
亦不女从。　　　　　　　我也不会顺从你。

羔 羊

羔羊之皮，　　　　　　　羔羊皮做袄，
素丝五紽②。　　　　　　白丝交错缝。
退食自公，　　　　　　　退朝吃饭在公家，
委蛇委蛇③。　　　　　　步履神态全从容。

---

① 室家：成室成家，结婚。
② 五紽（tuó）：丝线交错缝制。
③ 委蛇：从容自得。

Who says in sparrow's head
No beak can pierce the roof?
Who says the man's not wed?
He jails me without proof.
He can't wed me in jail;
I'm jailed to no avail.

Who says in the rat's head
No teeth can pierce the wall?
Who says the man's not wed?
He brings me to judge's hall.
Though brought to judge's hall.
I will not yield at all.

Officials in Lamb Furs①

In lamb and sheep skins drest,
With their five braidings white,
They come from court to rest
And swagger with delight.

---

① It was said that this song was a satire on those officials who did nothing but swagger, take meals and rest without delight.

羔羊之革，	羔羊革做袄，
素丝五緎。	白丝交错缝。
委蛇委蛇，	步履神态全从容，
自公退食。	退朝吃饭也在公。

羔羊之缝①，	羔羊皮做袄，
素丝五总。	白丝交错缝。
委蛇委蛇，	步履神态全从容，
退食自公。	退朝吃饭也在公。

殷②其雷

殷其雷，	隆隆的雷声，
在南山之阳。	就在南山的阳坡。
何斯违斯③？	为什么又要离开这里？
莫敢或遑④。	不敢稍有停留。
振振君子，	诚实忠厚的君子，
归哉归哉！	归来啊归来吧！

殷其雷，	隆隆的雷声，
在南山之侧。	在南山的旁边。
何斯违斯？	为什么又要离开这里？
莫敢遑息。	不敢稍事歇息。

---

① 缝：革。
② 殷（yīn）：雷声。
③ 违斯：离开此地。
④ 遑：闲暇。

In sheep and lamb skins drest,
With five seams of silk white,
They swagger, come to rest
And take meals with delight.

In lamb and sheep furs drest,
With their five joinings white,
They take their meals and rest
And swagger with delight.

Why Not Return?[①]

The thunder rolls away
O'er southern mountain's crest.
Why far from home do you stay,
Not daring take a rest?
Brave lord for whom I yearn,
Return, return!

The thunder rolls away
By southern mountain's side.
Why far from home do you stay,
Not daring take a ride?

[①] A young wife was longing for the return of her husband absent on public service.

振振君子, 　　诚实忠厚的君子,
归哉归哉! 　　归来啊归来吧!

殷其雷, 　　隆隆的雷声,
在南山之下, 　　在南山的下边。
何斯违斯? 　　为什么又要离开这里?
莫敢遑处。 　　不敢稍作闲处。
振振君子, 　　诚实忠厚的君子,
归哉归哉! 　　归来啊归来吧!

摽①有梅

摽有梅, 　　梅子纷纷落地,
其实七兮。 　　还有七成在树。
求我庶②士, 　　追求我的士子们,
迨③其吉兮! 　　不要误了好日子!

摽有梅, 　　梅子纷纷落地,
其实三兮, 　　还有三成在树。
求我庶士, 　　追求我的士子们,
迨其今兮! 　　今天就是好日子!

---

① 摽（biào）：落下。
② 庶：众多。
③ 迨：及时。

Brave lord for whom I yearn,
Return, return!

The thunder rolls away
At southern mountain's foot.
Why far from home do you stay
As if you'd taken root?
Brave lord for whom I yearn,
Return, return!

An Old Maid[①]

The fruits from mume-tree fall,
One-third of them away.
If you love me at all,
Woo me a lucky day!

The fruits from mume-tree fall,
Two-thirds of them away.
If you love me at all,
Woo me this very day!

---

① According to ancient custom, young people should be married in spring. When mume fruit fell, it was summer and maidens over twenty might get married without courtship.

摽有梅,
顷筐墍①之。
求我庶士,
迨其谓之!

梅子纷纷落地,
要用筐来收取了。
追求我的士子们,
姑娘就等你开口!

小 星

嘒②彼小星,
三五在东。
肃肃③宵征,
夙夜在公。
寔命不同!

小星微微闪着光,
三三五五在东方。
急急夜里来赶路,
为了公事早晚忙。
实在命运不一样!

嘒彼小星,
维参与昴。
肃肃宵征,
抱衾与裯。
寔命不犹!

小星微微闪着光,
参星靠在昴星旁。
急急夜里来赶路,
被子帐子自己扛。
真是人人比我强!

① 墍(jì):收取。
② 嘒:微光。
③ 肃肃:急速匆忙。

The fruits from mume-tree fall,
Now all of them away.
If you love me at all,
You need not woo but say.

The Starlets[1]

Three or five stars shine bright
Over the eastern gate.
We make haste day and night,
Busy early and late.
Different is our fate.

The starlets shed weak light
With the Pleiades o'erhead.
We make haste day and night,
Carrying sheets of bed:
No other way instead.

---

[1] This was a complaint of petty officials who should get up by starlight and go to bed by starlight.

江有汜[1]

江有汜,　　　　　　　　大江也有水分流,
之子归,　　　　　　　　夫君归来是时候,
不我以。　　　　　　　　他不亲近我。
不我以,　　　　　　　　他不亲近我,
其后也悔。　　　　　　　他的懊悔在后头。
江有渚,　　　　　　　　大江也有小水洲,
之子归,　　　　　　　　夫君归来是时候,
不我与。　　　　　　　　他不同我聚。
不我与,　　　　　　　　他不同我聚,
其后也处!　　　　　　　他的忧愁在后头。

江有沱[2],　　　　　　　大江也会有支流,
之子归。　　　　　　　　夫君归来是时候,
不我过。　　　　　　　　他不到我处。
不我过,　　　　　　　　他不到我处,
其啸也歌。　　　　　　　以哭当歌在后头。

[1] 汜:由主流分出而后汇合的河流。
[2] 沱:江的支流。

A Merchant's Wife[1]

Upstream go you
To wed the new
And leave the old,
You leave the old:
Regret foretold.
Downstream go you
To wed the new
And forsake me.
You forsake me;
Rueful you'll be.

Bystream go you
To wed the new
And desert me.
You desert me.
Woeful you'll be.

---

[1] This was the complaint of a woman deserted by her husband who went upstream and downstream for commerce.

野有死麕[1]

野有死麕,　　　　　　　打死的獐子郊在地,
白茅包之。　　　　　　白茅草包起它。
有女怀春,　　　　　　有个姑娘动了心,
吉士[2]诱之。　　　　　小伙子趁机讨好她。

林有朴樕[3],　　　　　树林里伐倒小树,
野有死鹿,　　　　　　野地里躺着死鹿,
白茅纯束[4]。　　　　　白茅草搓绳一起捆。
有女如玉。　　　　　　有个姑姑美如玉。

"舒而脱脱[5]兮,　　　缓缓地慢慢来,
无感我帨[6]兮!　　　　别碰得我围裙动!
无使尨[7]也吠!"　　　别惹得那狗儿叫。

何彼襛矣[8]

何彼襛矣?　　　　　　怎么那样绚艳繁盛?
唐棣之华。　　　　　　像郁李的花一样。

① 麕:獐鹿。
② 吉士:男子的美称。
③ 朴樕:小树。
④ 纯(tún)束:捆扎。
⑤ 脱脱(duì duì):慢慢地。
⑥ 帨:围裙。
⑦ 尨(máng):多毛狗。
⑧ 襛:繁盛的样子。

A Deer Killer and a Jadelike Maiden[①]

An antelope is killed
And wrapped in white afield.
A maid for love does long,
Tempted by a hunter strong.

He cuts down trees amain
And kills a deer again.
He sees the white-drest maid
As beautiful as jade.

"O soft and slow, sweetheart,
Don't tear my sash apart!"
The jadelike maid says, "Hark!
Do not let the dog bark!"

The Princess' Wedding[②]

Luxuriant in spring
As plum flowers o'er water,

[①] A hunter killed a deer, wrapped it in white rushes and offered it as present to a beautiful maiden. The last stanza described their lovemaking implicitly.
[②] This song described the marriage in 683 B. C. of the granddaughter of King Ping (769—719 B. C.) and the son of the Marquise of Qi. The silken thread forming a fishing line might allude to the newly-wed forming a happy family.

曷不肃雍，　　　　　　　　多么雍容又大方，
王姬之车。　　　　　　　　那是王姬的花车。

何彼秾矣？　　　　　　　　怎么那么绚艳繁盛？
华如桃李。　　　　　　　　盛放的桃李般漂亮。
平王之孙，　　　　　　　　那是平王的孙女，
齐侯之子。　　　　　　　　齐侯儿子是新郎。

其钓维何？　　　　　　　　用什么钓鱼最适宜？
维丝伊缗①。　　　　　　　用丝麻搓合成钓绳。
齐侯之子，　　　　　　　　那是齐侯的儿郎，
平王之孙。　　　　　　　　平王的孙女结婚姻。

驺 虞

彼茁者葭②，　　　　　　　丛生的芦苇真茁壮，
壹发五豝③。　　　　　　　一箭射中五头大猪。
于嗟乎驺④虞！　　　　　　好样的猎人啊！

彼茁者蓬，　　　　　　　　茁壮的蓬蒿做箭干，
壹发五豵⑤。　　　　　　　一箭射中五只小猪。
于嗟乎驺虞！　　　　　　　好样的猎人啊！

① 缗：绳。
② 葭：芦苇。
③ 豝（bā）：母猪。
④ 驺虞：猎人。
⑤ 豵（zōng）：小猪。

How we revere the string
Of cabs for the king's daughter!

Luxuriant in spring
As the peach flowers red,
The daughter of the king
To a marquis' son is wed.

we use the silken thread
To form a fishing line.
The son of marquis is wed
To the princess divine.

A Hunter[1]

Abundant rushes grow along;
One arrow hits one boar among.
Ah! What a hunter strong!

Abundant reeds along the shores,
One arrow scares five boars.
Ah! What a hunter one adores!

---

[1] This was a song sung during the hunting season in spring.

邶　风

柏　舟

泛^①彼柏舟，	柏木船儿顺水流，
亦泛其流。	漂漂荡荡不停休。
耿耿^②不寐，	心内不安难入眠，
如有隐忧。	如有烦恼在心头。
微我无酒，	不是家中没有酒，
以敖以游。	遨游也难消我愁。
我心匪鉴^③，	我心并非明镜，
不可以茹^④。	不是所有都留影。
亦有兄弟，	我兄我弟全都在，
不可以据。	依靠信任都不行。
薄言往愬，	正要去向其诉说，
逢彼之怒。	他们却在发雷霆。
我心匪石，	我心不能石头般，
不可转也。	哪能随人来翻转。
我心匪席，	我心难把芦席比，
不可卷也。	哪能任人翻卷起。

① 泛：随水流动。
② 耿耿：烦躁不安的样子。
③ 鉴：镜子。
④ 茹：容纳，含影。

Songs Collected in Bei, Modern Hebei

Depression[1]

Like cypress boat
Mid-stream afloat,
I cannot sleep
In sorrow deep.
I won't drink wine,
Nor roam nor pine.

Unlike the brass
Where images pass,
On brothers I
Cannot rely.
When I complain,
I meet disdain.

Have I not grown
Firm as a stone?
Am I as flat
As level mat?

---

[1] This song may be interpreted either as complaint of a man or of a woman. Some say it was the forerunner of Departure in Sorrow by Qu Yuan (340—278 B. C.).

威仪棣棣①，	堂正雍容有威仪，
不可选②也。	不能退避受挑剔。

忧心悄悄③，	忧愁烦恼备煎熬，
愠于群小。	小人憎恨也不少。
觏④闵⑤既多，	遭逢痛苦既已多，
受侮不少。	忍受侮辱更不少。
静言思之，	细细想起这些事，
寤辟有摽。	捶胸顿足心如搅。

日居月诸⑥，	太阳啊月亮啊，
胡迭而微⑦？	为何总有无光时？
心之忧矣，	心里忧愁忘不了，
如匪浣衣。	如同没洗脏衣服。
静言思之，	细细想起这些事，
不能奋飞。	不能奋翅高飞翔。

① 棣棣：堂堂正正，雍容闲雅。
② 选：指责挑剔。
③ 悄悄：忧愁的样子。
④ 觏：遭遇。
⑤ 闵：忧患。
⑥ 诸：语气助词，无实义。
⑦ 微：昏暗无光。

My mind is strong:
I've done no wrong.

I'm full of spleen,
Hated by the mean;
I'm in distress,
Insulted no less;
Thinking at rest,
I beat my breast.

The sun and moon
Turn dim so soon,
I'm in distress
Like dirty dress.
Silent think l:
Why can't I fly?

绿 衣

绿兮衣①兮，　　　　　　　绿色衣啊绿色衣，
绿衣黄里②。　　　　　　　绿色外衣黄色里。
心之忧矣，　　　　　　　　心里忧伤心忧伤啊，
曷维其已！　　　　　　　　何时才能够停止！

绿兮衣兮，　　　　　　　　绿色衣啊绿色衣，
绿衣黄裳③。　　　　　　　绿色外衣黄裙裳。
心之忧矣，　　　　　　　　心里忧伤心忧伤啊，
曷维其亡！　　　　　　　　何时才能够遗忘！

绿兮丝兮，　　　　　　　　绿色丝啊绿色丝，
女所治兮。　　　　　　　　你曾亲手所缝制。
我思古人④，　　　　　　　想我亡故的贤妻啊，
俾⑤无讹兮。　　　　　　　使我平生少过失。

絺兮绤兮，　　　　　　　　葛布不论粗和细啊，
凄其以风。　　　　　　　　穿在身上凉凄凄。
我思古人，　　　　　　　　想我亡故的贤妻啊，
实获我心。　　　　　　　　真正是合我心意。

① 衣：上衣。
② 里：上衣的衬里。
③ 裳：下衣。
④ 古人：即"故人"，指已死去的妻子。
⑤ 俾：使。

My Green Robe[①]

My upper robe is green;
Yellow my lower dress
My sorrow is so keen;
When will end my distress?

My upper robe is green;
Yellow my dress with dots.
My sorrow is so keen;
How can it be forgot?

The silk is green that you,
Old mate, dyed all night long;
I miss you, old mate, who
Kept me from doing wrong.

The linen coarse or fine
Is cold when blows the breeze.
I miss old mate of mine,
Who put my mind at ease.

① This was the first elegy in which a widower missed his deceased wife who had made the green robe and yellow dress for him.

燕　燕

燕燕于飞，	燕子飞来飞去，
差池①其羽。	羽翅参差不齐。
之子于归，	我的妹子要远嫁，
远送于野。	送到郊外要分手。
瞻望弗及，	眺望踪影不能见，
泣涕如雨。	涕泪如雨落纷纷。
燕燕于飞，	燕子飞来飞去，
颉之颃②之。	上下相随呢喃唱。
之子于归，	我的妹子要远嫁，
远于将之。	远远相送道路长。
瞻望弗及，	眺望踪影不能见，
伫立以泣。	呆立流泪心悲伤。
燕燕于飞，	燕子飞来飞去，
下上其音。	鸣声呢喃时翻飞。
之子于归，	我的妹子要远嫁，
远送于南。	送她远嫁去南方。
瞻望弗及，	眺望踪影不能见，
实劳我心。	思念不已心悲伤。

① 差池：不整齐。
② 颉、颃（háng）：上下飞舞。

A Farewell Song[1]

A pair of swallows fly
With their wings low and high.
You go home in your car;
I see you off afar.
When your car disappears,
Like rain fall down my tears.

A pair of swallows fly;
You go home with a sigh.
When they fly up and down,
I see you leave the town.
When your car disappears,
I stand there long in tears.

A pair of swallows fly,
Their songs heard far and nigh.
You go to your home state;
I see you leave south gate.
When your car disappears.
Deeply grieved, I shed tears.

[1] This was the first farewell song in Chinese history, written by Duchess Zhuang Jiang whose beauty was described in Poem "The Duke's Bride" and who bore no children but brought up the son of Duchess Dai Wei, who became Duke Huan of Wei and was murdered by his half brother on the 16th day of the 3rd moon in 719 B. C. In this farewell song the duchess related her grief at the departure of Duchess Dai Wei, obliged to return to her native State of Chen after her son's death. The "late lord" here refers to their husband.

仲①氏任②只，　　　　　　二妹诚实且可靠，
其心塞渊。　　　　　　　思虑沉稳远深长。
终温且惠，　　　　　　　心性温和又恭顺，
淑慎其身。　　　　　　　为人谨慎又善良。
先君之思，　　　　　　　如此安排是先君，
以勖③寡人④。　　　　　　以此勉慰我忧伤。

日 月

日居月诸，　　　　　　　太阳啊月亮啊，
照临下土。　　　　　　　光辉普照大地上。
乃如之人兮！　　　　　　怎么能有这样的人！
逝不古处。　　　　　　　会把古道全相忘。
胡能有定？　　　　　　　心内亡念何以止？
宁不我顾？　　　　　　　为何竟然把我忘？

日居月诸，　　　　　　　太阳啊月亮啊，
下土是冒⑤。　　　　　　光辉普照大地上。
乃如之人兮！　　　　　　怎么能有这样的人！
逝不相好。　　　　　　　义断情绝不来往。
胡能有定？　　　　　　　心内妄念何以止？
宁不我报？　　　　　　　为何让我空相望？

① 仲：排行第二。
② 任：信赖可靠。
③ 勖：勉励。
④ 寡人：寡德之人。
⑤ 冒：覆盖。

My faithful sister dear
With feeling e'er sincere,
So gentle and so sweet,
So prudent and discreet!
The thought of our late lord
Strikes our sensitive chord.

Sun And Moon[①]

Sun and moon bright,
Shed light on earth!
This man in sight
Without true worth
Has set his mind
To be unkind.

Sun and moon bright,
Cast shade with glee!
This man in sight
Would frown at me.
He's set his mind
To leave me behind.

① This song was the complaint of a wife abandoned by her husband.

日居月诸，	太阳啊月亮啊，
出自东方。	闪烁光辉出东方。
乃如之人兮！	怎么能有这样的人！
德音无良。	胡言乱语丧天良。
胡能有定？	心内妄念何以止？
俾也可忘。	使我难于把他忘。
日居月诸，	太阳啊月亮啊，
东方自出。	东方升起天下亮。
父兮母兮！	唤罢父亲喊母亲啊！
畜①我不卒。	夫君养我不久长。
胡能有定？	心内妄念何以止？
报我不述！	待我全无道理讲！

终 风

终风②且暴，	狂风吹得大又急，
顾我则笑。	见了我就笑嘻嘻。
谑浪笑敖，	对我戏谑又讪笑，
中心是悼！	我的心里生烦恼！

① 畜：养育。
② 终风：整天刮风。

Sun and moon bright
Rise from the east.
This man in sight
Is worse than beast.
His mind is set
All to forget.

Sun and moon bright
From east appear.
Can I requite
My parents dear?
My mind not set,
Can I forget?

The Violent Wind[①]

The wind blows violently;
He looks and smiles at me.
With me he seems to flirt;
My heart feels deeply hurt.

---

① This is the description of a feminine mind after a man's flirtation with her.

终风且霾①,　　　　　　　狂风大作尘飞扬,
惠然肯来?　　　　　　　难道他能来光顾?
莫往莫来,　　　　　　　如他不来往,
悠悠我思!　　　　　　　我又总是把他想!

终风且曀②,　　　　　　　整天刮风又阴天,
不日有曀。　　　　　　　不见太阳黑沉沉。
寤言不寐,　　　　　　　翻来覆去睡不着,
愿言则嚏③。　　　　　　想得使他打喷嚏。

曀曀其阴,　　　　　　　黑黑沉沉天阴阴,
虺虺其雷。　　　　　　　轰轰隆隆正打雷。
寤言不寐,　　　　　　　翻来覆去睡不着,
愿言则怀。　　　　　　　但愿他也能想我。

击 鼓

击鼓其镗④,　　　　　　　敲击战鼓镗镗响,
踊跃用兵⑤。　　　　　　士兵踊跃练刀枪。
土国城漕,　　　　　　　别人修路筑城墙,
我独南行。　　　　　　　独我从军到南方。

① 霾:阴尘。
② 曀:阴沉。
③ 嚏:打喷嚏。
④ 镗:击鼓的声音。
⑤ 兵:兵器。

The wind blows dustily;
He's kind to come to me.
Should he nor come nor go.
How would my yearning grow!

The wind blows all the day;
The clouds won't fly away.
Awake, I'm ill at ease.
Would he miss me and sneeze!

In gloomy cloudy sky
The thunder rumbles high.
I cannot sleep again.
O would he know my pain!

Complaint of a Soldier[①]

The drums are booming out;
We leap and bound about.
We build walls high and low,
But I should southward go.

---

① A soldier of the State of Wei repined over his separation form his family after the war made on the State of Chen in 718 B. C.

从孙子仲，	跟随将军孙子仲，
平①陈与宋。	交好盟国陈与宋。
不我以归，	驻守南方不能归，
忧心有忡。	我心伤悲有苦痛。
爰居爰处？	在哪儿住啊在哪儿歇？
爰丧其马？	在哪儿失了我的马？
于以求之？	去往哪里寻找它？
于林之下。	树林大树下。
"死生契阔②"，	"生死永远不分离"，
与子成说③。	我曾与你相盟定。
执子之手，	当时握着你的手，
与子偕老。	发誓到死不分离。
于嗟阔兮，	可叹啊，如今相隔太遥远，
不我活兮！	我们不能重相聚。
于嗟洵兮，	可叹啊，如今离别太长久，
不我信④兮！	我们不能守誓言。

① 平：和好，交好。
② 契阔：契合疏阔。
③ 成说：约定，成约。
④ 信：伸。

We follow Sun Zizhong
To fight with Chen and Song.
I cannot homeward go;
My heart is full of woe.

Where stop and stay our forces
When we have lost our horses?
Where can we find them, please?
Buried among the trees.

Meet or part, live or die;
We made oath, you and I.
When can our hands we hold
And live till we grow old?
Alas! So long we've parted,
Can I live broken-hearted?
Alas! The oath we swore
Can be fulfilled no more.

凯 风①

凯风自南，	和风吹来自南方，
吹彼棘心②。	吹在酸枣树苗上。
棘心夭夭，	酸枣树苗还正小，
母氏劬③劳。	母亲辛苦又勤劳。

凯风自南，	和风吹来自南方，
吹彼棘薪。	吹在酸枣枝条上。
母氏圣善，	母亲明理又善良，
我无令人④。	我们兄弟不像样。

爰有寒泉。	寒泉清冷把暑消，
在浚之下。	源在浚城之下绕。
有子七人，	儿子七个不算少，
母氏劳苦。	母亲依旧独勤劳。
睍睆⑤黄鸟，	美丽黄鸟，
载好其音。	婉转和鸣。
有子七人，	空有七子，
莫慰母心。	不能安慰慈母心。

① 凯风：和风。
② 棘心：小酸枣树。
③ 劬（qú）：辛勤。
④ 令人：善人，好样的。
⑤ 睍睆（xiàn huǎn）：美丽，漂亮。

Our Mother[①]

From the south blows the breeze
Amid the jujube trees.
The trees grow on the soil;
We live on mother's toil.

From the south blows the breeze
On branches of the trees.
Our mother's good to sons;
We are not worthy ones.

The fountain's water runs
To feed the stream and soil.
Our mother's seven sons
Are fed by her hard toil.
The yellow birds can sing
To comfort us with art.
We seven sons can't bring
Comfort to mother's heart

① Seven sons blamed themselves for the unhappiness of their mother in her state of widowhood.

雄 雉[①]

雄雉于飞,　　　　　　　　雄雉展翅飞远方,
泄泄[②]其羽。　　　　　　拍拍翅膀真舒畅。
我之怀矣,　　　　　　　　想念无止境,
自诒[③]伊阻[④]!　　　　　独留空忧伤!

雄雉于飞,　　　　　　　　雄雉展翅飞远方,
下上其音。　　　　　　　　上下翻飞自鸣唱。
展[⑤]矣君子,　　　　　　诚实我君子,
实劳我心!　　　　　　　　牵挂心难放!

瞻彼日月,　　　　　　　　眼看日月向人催,
悠悠我思!　　　　　　　　忧愁思念更悠长。
道之云远,　　　　　　　　道路相隔太遥远,
曷云能来?　　　　　　　　何时回到我身旁?

百尔[⑥]君子,　　　　　　所谓君子都一样,
不知德行。　　　　　　　　没有道德与修养。
不忮[⑦]不求,　　　　　　如若不妒且又不贪,
何用不臧[⑧]?　　　　　　走到哪里都顺畅?

① 雉:野鸡。
② 泄泄:慢慢舒展。
③ 诒:留。
④ 阻:忧伤。
⑤ 展:诚实。
⑥ 百尔:众多。
⑦ 忮(zhì):损人,害人。
⑧ 臧:顺利。

My Man in Service*[1]

The male pheasant in flight
Wings its way left and right.
O dear one of my heart!
We are so far apart.

See the male pheasant fly;
Hear his song low and high.
My man is so sincere.
Can I not miss him so dear?

Gazing at moon or sun,
I think of my dear one.
The way's a thousand li.
How can he come to me?

If he is really good,
He will do what he should.
For nothing would he long.
Will he do anything wrong?

---

[1] A wife deplored the absence of her husband in service and celebrated his virtue.

匏^①有苦叶

匏有苦叶，　　　　　　　　葫芦叶子枯萎，
济有深涉。　　　　　　　　济水深处也能渡。
深则厉^②，　　　　　　　水深漫着衣裳行，
浅则揭^③。　　　　　　　水浅提起衣裳过。

有弥济盈，　　　　　　　　茫茫白水济河满，
有鹭^④雉鸣。　　　　　　野鸡吆吆声不断。
济盈不濡轨，　　　　　　　水满不过半轮高，
雉鸣求其牡。　　　　　　　雌鸡把那雄鸡叫。

雝雝^⑤鸣雁，　　　　　　雁鸣声声真相和，
旭日始旦。　　　　　　　　初升太阳照济河。
士如归妻，　　　　　　　　你若有心来娶我，
迨冰未泮^⑥。　　　　　　莫等封冰早过河。

招招舟子，　　　　　　　　船夫摇摇把船摆，
人涉卬^⑦否。　　　　　　别人过河我等待。
人涉卬否，　　　　　　　　别人过河我等待，
卬须我友。　　　　　　　　等个人儿过河来。

① 匏：葫芦。
② 厉：以衣涉水。
③ 揭（qì）：提起衣裳渡水。
④ 鹭（yǎo）：野鸡的叫声。
⑤ 雝雝：雁鸣声。
⑥ 泮：冰化成水。
⑦ 卬：我。

Waiting for Her Fiance[①]

The gourd has leaves which fade;
The stream's too deep to wade.
If shallow leap
And strip if deep!

See the stream's water rise;
Hear female pheasant's cries.
The stream wets not the axle straight;
The pheasant's calling for her mate.

Hear the song of wild geese;
See the sun rise in glee.
Come before the streams freeze
If you will marry me.

I see the boatman row
Across but I will wait;
With others I won't go:
I will wait for my mate.

[①] A maiden was waiting at the ferry for her fiance to come across the stream.

谷风[1]

习习谷风,	呼呼吹来山谷风,
以阴以雨。	又是阴天又是雨。
黾勉[2]同心,	同心合意过日子,
不宜有怒。	不要对我发脾气。
采葑采菲,	采了萝卜和蔓菁,
无以下体?	为何根茎全抛弃?
德音莫违,	往日恩情休忘记,
及尔同死。	说好到死不分离。
行道迟迟,	踏上去路慢腾腾,
中心有违。	心里有恨难移步。
不远伊迩,	只是几步不算远,
薄送我畿[3]。	只望送我到门坎。
谁谓荼苦,	谁说荼菜味道苦,
其甘如荠。	它的味比荠菜甜。
宴尔新昏,	你的新婚多快乐,
如兄如弟。	好比亲兄和亲弟。
泾以渭浊,	泾水因为渭水浑,
湜湜[4]其沚。	泾水停下也能清。
宴尔新昏,	你的新婚多快乐,

① 谷风:从山谷吹来的风。
② 黾(mǐn)勉:辛勤功劳。
③ 畿:门坎。
④ 湜湜(shí shí):水清澈见底。

A Rejected Wife[①]

Gently blows eastern breeze
With rain 'neath cloudy skies.
Let's set our mind to please
And let no anger rise!
Who gathers plants to eat
Should keep the root in view.
Do not forget what's meet
And me who'd die with you!

Slowly I go my way;
My heart feels sad and cold.
You go as far to say
Goodbye as the threshold.
Is lettuce bitter? Nay,
To me it seems e'en sweet.
Feasting on wedding day,
You two looks as brothers meet.

The by-stream is not clear,
Still we can see its bed.
Feasting your new wife dear,

---

① This was the plaint of a wife rejected and supplanted by another whom she addressed in lines 5—6 of the 3rd stanza.

不我屑以。	不屑跟我再亲近。
毋逝我梁,	不要放开我鱼梁,
毋发我笱。	不要打开我鱼筐。
我躬不阅,	自己尚且不能容,
遑①恤②我后?	身后事儿何暇想?
就其深矣,	河水深了,
方③之舟之。	用船用筏来渡它。
就其浅矣,	河水浅了,
泳之游之。	浮着游着来渡它。
何有何亡,	往日家产有或无,
黾勉求之。	尽心尽力去操持。
凡民④有丧,	左邻右舍有急难,
匍匐救之。	奔走扶助不拖延。
不我能慉⑤,	不再爱我未不恕,
反以我为雠。	反而把我当仇人。
既阻⑥我德⑦,	一片好心被你拒,
贾⑧用⑨不售⑩。	好似卖不出的货物。

① 遑:哪有空闲。
② 恤:忧念。
③ 方:用筏子渡河。
④ 民:左邻右舍的人。
⑤ 慉(xù):爱。
⑥ 阻:非难,拒绝。
⑦ 德:德惠,情意。
⑧ 贾:卖。
⑨ 用:中用的货物。
⑩ 不售:卖不出去。

You treat the old as dead.
Do not approach my dam,
Nor move my net away!
Rejected as I am,
What more have I to say?

When the river was deep,
I crossed by raft or boat;
When 't was shallow, I'd keep
Myself aswim or afloat.
I would have spared no breath
To get what we did need;
Wherever I saw death,
I would help with all speed.

You loved me not as mate;
Instead you gave me hell.
My virtue caused you hate
As wares which did not sell.

昔育①恐育鞫②，	从前日子太潦倒，
及尔颠覆。	相互扶持已度过。
既生既育，	现在生活更好转，
比予于毒。	却把我比大毒虫。

我有旨蓄，	我有干菜和腌菜，
亦以御冬。	可以用来过冬天。
宴尔新昏，	你们新婚很快乐，
以我御穷。	用我来抵御困穷。
有洸有溃③，	又是动粗又发怒，
既诒我肄④。	全家数我最辛苦。
不念昔者，	从前恩情你不念，
伊余来塈⑤。	我新来时亦爱浓。

式 微⑥

式微式微，	天色昏啊天将黑，
胡不归？	为什么却不回？
微⑦君之故，	不是因为君主的缘故，
胡为乎中露？	为什么全身遭受露水？

① 育：生活。
② 鞫：贫困潦倒。
③ 洸、溃：原指水激荡的样子，喻指人发怒动粗的样子。
④ 肄：辛苦的事情。
⑤ 塈（xì）：爱。
⑥ 微：通"昧"，此处指天色昏黄，夜幕将临。
⑦ 微：非，不是。

In days of poverty
Together we shared woe
Now in prosperity
I seem your poison slow.

I've vegetables dried
Against the winter cold.
Feast them with your new bride,
Not your former wife old.
You beat and scolded me
And gave me only pain.
The past is gone, I see,
And no love will remain.

Toilers[1]

It's near dusk, lo!
Why not home go?
It is for you
We're wet with dew.

---

[1] This was a plaint of toilers in the service of the marquis of Wei.

式微式微, 　　　　　　　　天色昏啊天将黑,
胡不归? 　　　　　　　　　为什么却不回?
微君之躬, 　　　　　　　　不是因为君主的身体,
胡为乎泥中? 　　　　　　　为什么全身沾满着泥水?

旄　丘 [1]

旄丘之葛兮, 　　　　　　　葛藤长在山坡上,
何诞之节兮? 　　　　　　　为何枝节那么长?
叔兮伯兮, 　　　　　　　　叔叔啊伯伯啊,
何多日也? 　　　　　　　　为何好久不帮忙?

何其处也? 　　　　　　　　在哪里安顿啊?
必有与也! 　　　　　　　　一定有帮助的人!
何其久也? 　　　　　　　　为何等这么久啊?
必有以也! 　　　　　　　　一定有它的原因!

狐裘蒙戎, 　　　　　　　　身穿狐裘毛纷乱,
匪车不东。 　　　　　　　　坐着车子不向东。
叔兮伯兮, 　　　　　　　　叔叔啊伯伯啊,
靡所与同。 　　　　　　　　我们感情不相通。

[1] 旄丘：前高后低的土山。

It's near dusk, lo!
Why not home go?
For you, O Sire,
We toil in mire.

Refugees[1]

The high mound's vines appear
So long and wide.
O uncles dear,
Why not come to our side?

Why dwell you thereamong
For other friends you make?
Why stay so long?
For who else' sake?

Furs in a mess appear;
Eastward goes not your cart.
O uncles dear,
Don't you feel sad at heart?

---

[1] It was said that this was a complaint of the refugees in the State of Wei.

琐兮尾①兮,　　　　　　　我们渺小又卑贱,
流离之子。　　　　　　　沦落流亡乞人怜。
叔兮伯兮,　　　　　　　叔叔啊伯伯啊,
褎②如充耳。　　　　　　趾高气扬听不见。

简 兮③

简兮简兮,　　　　　　　威武啊,气昂昂啊,
方将万舞④。　　　　　　看那万舞要开场。
日之方中,　　　　　　　太阳正在头顶上,
在前上处。　　　　　　　瞧他正在前面站。

硕人俣俣⑤,　　　　　　高高个子好身材,
公庭万舞。　　　　　　　公堂面前跳万舞。
有力如虎,　　　　　　　扮成力士力如虎,
执辔如组⑥。　　　　　　拿着缰绳如丝带。

左手执龠⑦,　　　　　　左手拿着管儿,
右手秉翟⑧。　　　　　　右手舞着雉羽。

---

① 尾:微。
② 褎(xiù):微笑。
③ 简:形容威容的姿态。
④ 万舞:古时一种用于朝廷、宗庙、山川祭祀仪式上的舞蹈,由文舞与武舞定合。
⑤ 俣俣(yǔ yǔ):大而美。
⑥ 组:宽丝带。
⑦ 龠(yuè):可以吹的一种乐器,似是排箫的前身。
⑧ 翟:野鸡尾。

So poor and base appear
We refugees.
O uncles dear,
Why don't you listen, please?

A Dancer[1]

With main and might
Dances the ace.
Sun at its height,
He holds his place.

He dances long
With might and main.
Like tiger strong
He holds the rein.

A flute in his left hand,
In his right a plume fine,

---

[1] It was said that this was a censure against the State of Wei for not giving offices equal to their merit to its men of worth but employing them as dancers.

赫如渥①赭②,　　　　　　　脸儿红得像赭石,
公言锡爵。　　　　　　　　大人赏赐一杯酒。

山有榛,　　　　　　　　　高高山上有榛栗,
隰③有苓。　　　　　　　　低田湿地长苦苓。
云谁之思?　　　　　　　　柔肠百结思念谁?
西方美人。　　　　　　　　来自西方的美人。
彼美人兮,　　　　　　　　那个美人啊,
西方之人兮。　　　　　　　正是来自西方啊。

泉　水

毖④彼泉水,　　　　　　　涓涓泉水流不息,
亦流于淇。　　　　　　　　最后流到淇水里。
有怀于卫,　　　　　　　　想起卫国我故乡,
靡日不思。　　　　　　　　没有一天不惦记。
娈彼诸姬,　　　　　　　　诸位姬姓好姐妹,
聊与之谋。　　　　　　　　姑且和她共商议。

① 渥:厚重
② 赭:赤褐色。
③ 隰:湿地。
④ 毖(bì):水流的样子。

Red-faced, he holds command,
Given a cup of wine.

Hazel above,
Sweet grass below.
Who is not sick for love
Of the dancing Beau?
Who is not sick for love
Of the Western Beau?

Fair Spring[①]

The bubbling water flows
From the spring to the stream.
My heart to homeland goes;
Day and night I seek to dream.
I'll ask my cousins dear
How I may start from here.

---

① A daughter of the House of Wei, married in another State, expressed her longing to revisit Wei.

出宿于泲①，	出门住宿在泲滨，
饮饯于祢。	喝酒饯行在祢城。
女子有行②，	姑娘出嫁到远方，
远父母兄弟。	离开兄弟和爹娘。
问我诸姑，	临行问候众姑姑，
遂及伯姊。	还有大姐别忘记。
出宿于干，	出门住宿在干地，
饮饯于言。	喝酒饯行在言城。
载脂载舝③，	涂好轴油安好键，
还车言迈。	转车回家走得快。
遄④臻⑤于卫，	只想快快回卫国，
不瑕有害？	回去看看又何妨？
我思肥泉，	想到那肥泉，
兹之永叹。	不免长声叹。
思须与漕，	想到须与漕，
我心悠悠。	心里长思念。
驾言出游，	驾车外出游，
以写我忧。	以此解我愁。

① 泲（jǐ）：与后面的祢、干、言，都是卫国的地名。
② 行：出嫁。
③ 舝（xiá）：车轴上的金属键。
④ 遄：快速地。
⑤ 臻：到。

I will lodge in one place,
Take my meal in another,
And try to find the trace
How I parted from mother.
I'll ask about aunts dear
On my way far from here.

I'll lodge in a third place
And dine in a fourth one.
I'll set my cab apace;
With axles greased 'twill run.
I'll hasten to go home.
Why should I not have come?

When I think of Fair Spring,
How can I not heave sighs!
Thoughts of my homeland bring
Copious tears to my eyes.
I drive to find relief
And drown my homesick grief.

北　门

出自北门	走出北门来，
忧心殷殷①。	心里忧愁意深深。
终窭②且贫，	一直鄙陋又贫困，
莫知我艰。	无人知道我艰难。
已焉哉！	算了吧！
天实为之，	老天这样的安排，
谓之何哉！	又有什么好说的！

王事适③我，	王事派给我，
政事一埤④益我。	公事加给我。
我入自外，	我从外面回家来，
室人交遍谪⑤我。	家人全都责备我。
已焉哉！	算了吧！
天实为之，	老天这样的安排，
谓之何哉！	又有什么好说的！

王事敦⑥我，	王事逼迫我，
政事一埤遗我。	公事加给我。

① 殷殷：忧愁的样子。
② 窭（jù）：鄙陋不能备礼。
③ 适：派给。
④ 埤（pí）：使。
⑤ 谪：责难，埋怨。
⑥ 敦：逼迫。

A Petty Official[1]

Out of north gate
Sadly I go.
I'm poor by fate.
Who knows my woe?
Let it be so!
Heaven wills this way.
What can I say?

I am busy about
Affairs of royalty.
When I come from without,
I'm blamed by family.
So let it be!
Heaven wills this way.
What can I say?

I am busier about
Public affairs, but oh!

---

[1] An officer of Wei set forth his hard lot and his silence under it in submission to Heaven.

我入自外,	我从外面回家,
室人交遍摧①我。	家人全都讽刺我。
已焉哉!	算了吧!
天实为之,	老天这样的安排,
谓之何哉!	又有什么好说的!

北 风

北风其凉,	北风吹得冷,
雨雪其雱②。	大雪下得猛。
惠而③好我,	我和我朋友,
携手同行。	握手一起走。
其虚④其邪⑤?	还能再磨蹭吗?
既⑥亟只且⑦!	情况很紧急啦!

北风其喈,	北风吹得响,
雨雪其霏。	大雪白茫茫。
惠而好我,	我和我朋友,
携手同归⑧。	握手一起走。
其虚其邪?	还能再磨蹭吗?
既亟只且!	情况很紧急啦!

① 摧:讽刺。
② 雱(pāng):下大雪的样子。
③ 惠而:仁爱相从。
④ 虚:即"舒"。
⑤ 邪:即"徐"。
⑥ 既:已经。
⑦ 只且:语气助词。
⑧ 同归:一起到有德的地方去。

When I come from without,
I'm given blow on blow.
Let it be so!
Heaven wills this way.
What can I say?

The Hard Pressed[①]

The cold north wind does blow
And thick does fall the snow.
To all my friends I say:
"Hand in hand let us go!
There's no time for delay;
We must hasten our way."

The sharp north wind does blow
And heavy falls the snow.
To all my friends I say
"Hand in hand let's all go!
There's no time for delay;
We must hasten our way."

---

① The hard-pressed people left the State of Wei in consequence of the prevailing oppression and misery. The first two lines in all the stanzas are a metaphorical description of the miserable condition of the State. Foxes and crows were both creatures of evil omen.

莫赤匪狐,　　　　　　　　没有红的不是狐狸,
莫黑匪乌。　　　　　　　　没有黑的不是乌鸦。
惠而好我,　　　　　　　　我和我朋友,
携手同车。　　　　　　　　握手同车走。
其虚其邪?　　　　　　　　还能再磨蹭吗?
既亟只且!　　　　　　　　情况很紧急啦!

静①女

静女其姝②,　　　　　　　　娴静的姑娘惹人爱,
俟我于城隅。　　　　　　　约我城角楼上来。
爱③而不见,　　　　　　　　暗地里藏着不见我,
搔首踟蹰④。　　　　　　　让我抓耳挠腮又徘徊。

静女其娈⑤,　　　　　　　　娴静的姑娘真美丽,
贻我彤管。　　　　　　　　送我彤管有用意。
彤管有炜⑥,　　　　　　　　彤管红红好光彩,
说怿⑦女美。　　　　　　　我是喜欢姑娘的美。

自牧归荑,　　　　　　　　送我白茅牧场采,
洵⑧美且异。　　　　　　　确实美丽不平凡。

① 静:娴静,端正庄重。
② 姝:美丽。
③ 爱:故意隐藏起来。
④ 踟蹰:徘徊的样子。
⑤ 娈:漂亮,美好。
⑥ 炜:红色鲜明有光泽。
⑦ 怿:喜爱。
⑧ 洵:确实,真的。

Red-handed foxes glow;
Their hearts are black as crow.
To all my friends I say
"In my cart let us go!
There's no time for delay;
We must hasten our way."

A Shepherdess[1]

A maiden mute and tall
Trysts me at corner wall.
I can find her nowhere;
Perplexed, I scratch my hair.

The maiden fair and mute
Gives me a grass-made lute.
Playing a rosy air,
I'm happier than e'er.

Coming back from the mead.
She gives me a rare reed,

---

[1] This was the first in Chinese song which the poet showed his participation in the feeling of things.

匪女之为美,   不是草儿太美丽,
美人之贻。   美人所赠心甜蜜。

新 台

新台有泚①,   新台照水倒影明,
河水弥弥②。   河水涨得与岸平。
燕婉③之求,   只说嫁个美少年,
籧篨④不鲜。   嫁个蛤蟆不像人。

新台有洒⑤,   新台近水建得高,
河水浼浼⑥。   河水涨满浪滔滔。
燕婉之求,   只说嫁个美少年,
籧篨不殄⑦。   嫁个蛤蟆不得了。

鱼网之设,   架起渔网为打鱼,
鸿⑧则离⑨之。   谁想打个癞蛤蟆。
燕婉之求,   只说嫁个美少年,
得此戚施⑩。   嫁个蛤蟆怎么办。

① 泚(cǐ):鲜明的样子。
② 弥弥:水盛大的样子。
③ 燕婉:安详和顺。
④ 籧篨(qú chú):蟾蜍,癞蛤蟆。
⑤ 洒(cuǐ):高峻的样子。
⑥ 浼浼(měi měi):水涨平岸。
⑦ 不殄:没福相。
⑧ 鸿:指蛤蟆。
⑨ 离:罹难,遭遇。
⑩ 戚施:蛤蟆。

Lovely not for it's rare:
It's given by the fair.

The New Tower[①]

How bright is the new tower
On brimming river deep!
Of youth she seeks the flower,
Not loathsome toad to keep.

How high is the new tower
On tearful river deep!
Of youth she seeks the flower,
No stinking toad to keep.

A net for fish is set;
A toad is caught instead.
The flower of youth she'll get,
Not a hunchback to wed.

[①] This was a satire against Duke Xuan of Wei who took his eldest son's bride as his own and built a new tower by the Yellow River to welcome her in 699 B. C. Here the toad and the hunchback refer to the duke and the flower of youth to his eldest son.

二子乘舟

二子乘舟,　　　　　　　　两位公子去坐船,
泛泛①其景。　　　　　　　漂漂荡荡去得远。
愿言思子,　　　　　　　　思念他们啊,
中心养养②。　　　　　　　心里忧愁不定当。

二子乘舟,　　　　　　　　两位公子去坐船,
泛泛其逝。　　　　　　　　漂漂荡荡去不还。
愿言思子,　　　　　　　　思念他们啊,
不瑕有害。　　　　　　　　该不会遭逢祸殃?

---

① 泛泛:飘荡。
② 养养:忧愁的样子。

Two Sons in a Boat[①]

My two sons take a boat;
Downstream their shadows float.
I miss them when they're out;
My heart is tossed about.

My two sons take a boat;
Far, far away they float.
I think of them so long.
Would no one do them wrong!

[①] Duke Xuan of Wei who had taken his eldest son's bride as his own plotted to get rid of this son by sinking his boat, but his younger brother, aware of this design, insisted on going in the same boat with him, and their mother, worried, wrote this song.

鄘 风

柏 舟

泛彼柏舟，	柏木船儿漂荡，
在彼中河。	在那河水中央。
髧①彼两髦②，	那人头发分两旁，
实维我仪③。	真是我的好对象。
之④死矢⑤靡它。	发誓到死无他心。
母也天只，	娘啊，天啊！
不谅人只！	我的心啊怎么就不体谅！
泛彼柏舟，	柏木船儿漂荡，
在彼河侧。	在那河水边上。
髧彼两髦，	那人头发分两旁，
实维我特⑥。	和我天生是一双。
之死矢靡慝⑦。	发誓到死不变心。
母也天只，	娘啊，天啊，
不谅人只！	怎么就不体谅我的心啊！

① 髧（dàn）：头发下垂的样子。
② 髦：把头发分成两股。
③ 仪：配偶，对象。
④ 之：到。
⑤ 矢：誓。
⑥ 特：配偶。
⑦ 慝（tè）：改变。

Songs Collected in Yong, Modern Shandong

A Cypress Boat[1]

A cypress boat
Midstream afloat.
Two tufts of hair o'er his forehead,
He is my mate to whom I'll wed.
I swear I won't change my mind till I'm dead.
Heaven and mother,
Why don't you understand another?

A cypress boat
By riverside afloat.
Two tufts of hair o'er his forehead,
He is my only mate to whom I'll wed.
I swear I won't change my mind though dead.
Heaven and mother,
Why don't you understand another?

---

[1] This song of a determined woman was mistaken for that of a chaste widow.

墙有茨①

墙有茨,　　　　　　　　　　墙上蒺藜草,
不可扫也。　　　　　　　　　不可把它扫。
中冓②之言,　　　　　　　　　宫廷悄悄话,
不可道也。　　　　　　　　　不可向外道。
所可道也,　　　　　　　　　如果向外道,
言之丑也。　　　　　　　　　说了让人臊。

墙有茨,　　　　　　　　　　墙上蒺藜草,
不可襄③也。　　　　　　　　不可尽除掉。
中冓之言,　　　　　　　　　宫中悄悄话,
不可详④也。　　　　　　　　不可仔细讲。
所可详也,　　　　　　　　　如果仔细讲,
言之长也。　　　　　　　　　要说话太长。

墙有茨,　　　　　　　　　　墙上蒺藜草,
不可束也。　　　　　　　　　不能都捆束。
中冓之言,　　　　　　　　　宫中悄悄话,
不可读也。　　　　　　　　　不可宣扬它。
所可读也,　　　　　　　　　如果要宣扬,
言之辱也。　　　　　　　　　说来是耻辱。

① 茨:蒺藜草。
② 中冓(gòu):宫闱内室。
③ 襄:除去。
④ 详:细说。

Scandals[①]

The creepers on the wall
Cannot be swept away.
Stories of inner hall
Should not be told by day.
What would have to be told
Is scandals manifold.

The creepers on the wall
Cannot be rooted out.
Scandals of inner hall
Should not be talked about.
If they are talked of long,
They'll be an endless song.

The creepers on the wall
Cannot be together bound.
Scandals of inner hall
Should not be spread around.
If spread from place to place,
They are shame and disgrace.

[①] After the death of Duke Xuan of Wei, the beautiful duchess had illicit connections with his son and gave birth to three sons and two daughters, the youngest daughter being Baroness Mu of Xu who wrote the Poem "Patriotic Baroness Mu of Xu". These connections raised scandals in the inner hall of the ducal palace.

君子偕老

君子偕老,　　　　　　　　　宣公和你同到老,
副①笄②六珈③。　　　　　　首饰玉簪镶珠宝。
委委佗佗,　　　　　　　　　体态庄重又从容,
如山如河,　　　　　　　　　思如河深体如崇,
象服④是宜。　　　　　　　　身上华服很合适。
子之不淑⑤,　　　　　　　　你的德行不贤淑,
云如之何?　　　　　　　　　还能让人如何讲?

玼⑥兮玼兮,　　　　　　　　真鲜艳啊又绚丽,
其之翟⑦也。　　　　　　　　绣着雉纹的翟衣。
鬒⑧发如云,　　　　　　　　黑发如云真正美,
不屑髢⑨也。　　　　　　　　不必用那假发佩。
玉之瑱⑩也,　　　　　　　　美玉耳环垂两边,
象之揥⑪也,　　　　　　　　象牙簪子插发间,
扬⑫且之皙也。　　　　　　　额头宽广又白皙。

---

① 副：古代女人的首饰。
② 笄：簪子。
③ 珈：首饰名，又称步摇。
④ 象服：画袍，是王后之服。
⑤ 不淑：不幸。
⑥ 玼（cǐ）：玉色鲜明。
⑦ 翟：翟衣，祭服，绣绘有翟雉之形。
⑧ 鬒（zhěn）：黑发。
⑨ 髢（dí）：假发。
⑩ 瑱（tiàn）：垂在两耳旁的玉。
⑪ 揥（tì）：发插类的首饰。
⑫ 扬：眉宇间开阔方正。

Duchess Xuan Jiang of Wei[1]

She'd live with her lord till old,
Adorned with gems and gold.
Stately and full of grace,
Stream-like, she went her pace.
As a mountain she'd dwell;
Her robe became her well.
Raped by the father of her lord,
O how could she not have been bored!

She is so bright and fair
In pheasant-figured gown.
Like cloud is her black hair,
No false locks but her own.
Her earrings are of jade,
Her pin ivory-made.

[1] This was a portrait of the beautiful Duchess Xuan of Wei. The first stanza described her arrival at the new tower (See Poem "The New Tower").

胡然而天也?	莫非尘世有天仙?
胡然而帝也?	莫非帝子降人间?
瑳①兮瑳兮,	真美丽啊真明艳,
其之展②也,	轻薄细纱做礼服,
蒙彼绉絺③,	罩上蝉翼般纹衣,
是绁袢④也。	夏天穿着白内衣。
子之清扬,	你的眉目清且秀,
扬且之颜也。	额头丰满又白净。
展⑤如之人兮,	的的确确这个人,
邦之媛也!	倾城倾国的美女啊!

桑 中

爰采唐⑥矣?	什么地方把那菟丝子采?
沬之乡矣。	在那沬邑的郊外。
云谁之思?	想念的那人儿是谁?
美孟⑦姜矣。	美丽的姜家大姑娘。
期我乎桑中,	约我等待在桑田,
要我乎上宫,	邀我相会在上宫,
送我乎淇之上矣。	淇水边上长相送。

① 瑳：玉色洁白鲜明。
② 展：夏天的礼服。
③ 绉絺（chī）：细葛布。
④ 绁袢：夏天穿白色内衣。
⑤ 展：诚然，的确。
⑥ 唐：菟丝子草。
⑦ 孟：兄弟姐妹中排行最长的人。

Her forehead's white and high,
Like goddess from the sky.

She is so fair and bright
In rich attire snow-white.
O'er her fine undershirt
She wears close-fitting skirt.
Her eyes are bright and clear;
Her face will facinate.
Alas! Fair as she might appear,
She's a raped beauty of the State.

Trysts[①]

"Where gather golden thread?"
"In the fields over there."
"Of whom do you think ahead?"
"Jiang's eldest daughter fair.
She did wait for me 'neath mulberry,
In upper bower tryst with me
And see me off on River Qi."

[①] It was possible that this song was constructed to deride the licentiousness that prevailed in the State of Wei.

爰采麦矣？	什么地方把那麦穗采？
沬之北矣。	在那沬邑的北边。
云谁之思？	想念的那人儿是谁？
美孟弋矣。	美丽的弋家大姑娘。
期我乎桑中，	约我等待在桑田，
要我乎上宫，	邀我相会在上宫，
送我乎淇之上矣。	淇水边上长相送。

爰采葑矣？	什么地方把那芜菁采？
沬之东矣。	在那沬邑的东边。
云谁之思？	想念的那人儿是谁？
美孟庸矣。	美丽的庸家大姑娘。
期我乎桑中，	约我等待在桑田，
要我乎上宫，	邀我相会在上宫，
送我乎淇之上矣。	淇水边上长相送。

鹑[①]之奔奔[②]

鹑之奔奔，	雌鹑跟着雄鹑飞，
鹊之强强[③]。	雌鹊跟着雄鹊飞。
人之无良，	这个男人不善良，
我以为兄。	为啥当他是兄长。

[①] 鹑：鹌鹑。
[②] 奔奔：雌雄同处同飞。
[③] 强强：同"奔奔"。

"Where gather golden wheat?"
"In northern fields o'er there."
"Whom do you long to meet?"
"Yi's eldest daughter fair.
She did wait for me 'neath mulberry,
In upper bower tryst with me
And see me off on River Qi."

"Where gather mustard plant?"
"In eastern fields o'er there."
"Who does your heart enchant?"
"Yong's eldest daughter fair.
She did wait for me 'neath mulberry,
In upper bower tryst with me
And see me off on River Qi."

Misfortune[1]

The quails together fly;
The magpies sort in pairs.
She takes an unkind guy
For brother unawares.

---

[1] The beautiful Duchess Xuan Jiang of Wei (See Poems "The New Tower", "Two Sons in a Boat Two Sons in a Boat", "Scandals", "Duchess Xuan Jiang of Wei") was first raped by Duke Xuan of Wei (master) and then by his son(brother). She was not so fortunate as quails and magpies which have a faithful mate.

鹊之强强，	雌鹊跟着雄鹊飞，
鹑之奔奔。	雌鹑跟着雄鹑飞。
人之无良，	这个男人不善良，
我以为君。	为啥当他是君王。

定①之方中②

定之方中，	营室星儿正当中，
作于楚宫。	十月修建楚邱宫。
揆③之以日，	确定方向察日影，
作于楚室。	建筑房屋兴工程。
树之榛栗，	种上榛树还有栗，
椅桐梓漆，	更有椅桐和梓漆，
爰伐琴瑟。	长成砍伐做琵琶。

升彼虚矣，	登上那个旧城址，
以望楚矣。	远眺楚邱的位置。
望楚与堂，	望见楚邱与堂邑，
景山④与京⑤。	大山高岗全相集。
降观于桑，	下来观察种桑地，
卜云其吉，	占卜都说大吉祥，
终然允⑥臧。	于是选中这福地。

① 定：星名，又名营室。
② 方中：正当中的位置。
③ 揆：测量。
④ 景山：大山。
⑤ 京：高冈。
⑥ 允：真正。

The magpies sort in pairs;
The quails together fly.
For master unawares
She takes an unkind guy.

Duke Wen of Wei[1]

At dusk the four stars form a square;
It's time to build a palace new.
The sun and shade determine where
To build the Palace at Chu,
To plant hazel and chestnut trees,
Fir, yew, plane, cypress. When cut down,
They may be used to make lutes to please The ducal crown.

The duke ascends the ruined wall
To view the site of capital
And where to build his palace hall.
He then surveys the mountain's height
And comes down to see mulberries.
The fortune-teller says it's right
And the duke is pleased with all these.

---

[1] After the defeat and death of Duke Yi of Wei in 659 B. C., Duke Wen succeeded him, moved the capital to Cao and built a new palace in Chu. As he was dilligent and sympathetic with the people, the State of Wei became prosperous under his reign.

灵雨既零,	好雨知时水如泉,
命彼倌①人。	命令那个驾车员。
星言夙驾,	从早到晚把车赶,
说②于桑田。	把车停歇在桑田。
匪直③也人,	不只关心把农劝,
秉心塞渊④,	诚心为国谋深远,
骐⑤牝⑥三千。	骏马繁殖到三千。

蝃蝀⑦

蝃蝀在东,	东方出彩虹,
莫之敢指。	没人敢指点它。
女子有行⑧,	姑娘要出嫁,
远父母兄弟。	远远离开父母兄弟家。
朝隮⑨于西,	早上虹云在西边,
崇朝⑩其雨。	整个早上在下雨。
女子有行,	姑娘要出嫁,
远兄弟父母。	远远离开父母兄弟家。

① 倌人:管理车马的小臣。
② 说:通"税",休息,停止。
③ 匪直:不但。
④ 塞渊:笃实深远。
⑤ 骐(lái):高大的马。
⑥ 牝:母马。
⑦ 蝃蝀(dì dōng):彩虹。
⑧ 行:出嫁。
⑨ 隮:彩云。
⑩ 崇朝:整个早晨。

After the fall of vernal rain
The duke orders his groom to drive
His horse and cab with might and main.
At mulberry fields they arrive;
To farmers he is good indeed
He wishes husbandry to thrive
And three thousand horses to breed.

Elopement[1]

A rainbow rose high in the east;
None dared to point to it at least.
I went to wed like others
And left my parents and my brothers.

The morning clouds rose in the west;
The day with rain would then be blest.
I went to wed another
When I left my father and mother.

---

[1] This was said to be a protest of Duchess Xuan Jiang against Duke Xuan of Wei who raped her (See Poem "Complaint of a Duchess"). A rainbow was regarded by ancient people as an emblem of improper connections between man and woman, and it was held unlucky to point to a rainbow in the east. The clouds bringing fresh showers to thirsting flowers were compared to love-making.

乃如之人也，　　　　　　她是这样的人儿啊，
怀昏姻也，　　　　　　　一心想着要出嫁。
大无信也，　　　　　　　不听媒妁之美言，
不知命也。　　　　　　　父母之命也不依。

相 鼠

相鼠有皮，　　　　　　　看看老鼠还有皮，
人而无仪①。　　　　　　这个人却没威仪。
人而无仪，　　　　　　　人要如果没威仪，
不死何为?　　　　　　　不死还能干什么?

相鼠有齿，　　　　　　　看看老鼠还有齿，
人而无止②。　　　　　　这个人却没节制。
人而无止，　　　　　　　人要如果没节制，
不死何俟?　　　　　　　不死还在等什么?

相鼠有体，　　　　　　　看看老鼠还有体，
人而无礼。　　　　　　　这个人却不守礼。
人而无礼。　　　　　　　人要如果不守礼法，
胡不遄③死。　　　　　　还不如快些就去死。

① 仪：威仪，使人尊敬的仪表。
② 止：言行适当，有所节制。
③ 遄：快速地。

Did I know I'd be raped by such a man
Who would do whatever he can!
He is a faithless mate.
Is it my fault or fate?

The Rat[①]

The rat has skin, you see?
Man must have decency.
If he lacks decency,
Worse than death it would be.

The rat has teeth, you see?
Man must have dignity.
If he lacks dignity,
For what but death waits he?

The rat has limbs, you see?
Man must have propriety.
Without propriety,
It's better dead to be.

---

① This was a satire against the ruling class of the State of Wei who, without propriety, was not equal to a rat.

干① 旄

孑孑②干旄,	旗杆上牛尾饰的旗,
在浚之郊。	树立在浚邑的郊区。
素丝纰③之,	白丝线把旗边缝,
良马四之。	四匹良马做前驱。
彼姝者子,	那们贤德的才俊,
何以畀④之?	拿什么送给他啊?

孑孑干旟,	旗杆上隼鸟纹饰的旗帜,
在浚之都。	树立在浚邑的都市。
素丝组之,	白丝线把旗边缝,
良马五之。	五匹良马做前驱。
彼姝者子,	那位贤德的才俊,
何以予之?	拿什么赠予他啊?

孑孑干旌,	旗杆上五色鸟羽饰的旗,
在浚之城。	树立在浚邑的城区。
素丝祝⑤之,	白丝线把旗边缝,
良马六之。	六匹良马做前驱。
彼姝者子,	那位贤德的才俊,
何以告之?	拿什么忠言以相告啊?

① 干:旗杆。
② 孑孑:特出的。
③ 纰:把旗的边上用线缝好。
④ 畀:给与。
⑤ 祝:连结。

Betrothal Gifts[①]

The flags with ox-tail tied
Flutter in countryside.
Adorned with silk bands white,
Four steeds trot left and right.
What won't I give and share
With such a maiden faire

The falcon-banners fly
In the outskirts nearby.
Adorned with ribbons white,
Five steeds trot left and right.
What won't I give and send
To such a good fair friend?

The feathered streamers go down
All the way to the town.
Bearing rolls of silk white,
Six steeds trot left and right.
What and how should I say
To her as fair as May?

[①] This song described how a young lord sent betrothal gifts to his fiancee.

载　驰

载驰载驱，　　　　　　　　赶着马儿快些走，
归唁①卫侯。　　　　　　　回来吊问我卫侯。
驱马悠悠②，　　　　　　　赶着马儿路悠悠，
言至于漕。　　　　　　　　走到漕邑城门楼。
大夫跋涉，　　　　　　　　许国大夫匆忙来，
我心则忧。　　　　　　　　让我心里添忧愁。

既不我嘉③，　　　　　　　对我做法都摇头，
不能旋反。　　　　　　　　可我不能往回走。
视尔不臧④，　　　　　　　你的想法不算好，
我思不远。　　　　　　　　我的做法近可求。

既不我嘉，　　　　　　　　对我做法都反对，
不能旋济。　　　　　　　　决不渡河再回头。
视尔不臧，　　　　　　　　你的想法不算好，
我思不閟⑤。　　　　　　　我的计划有理由。

陟彼阿丘，　　　　　　　　登上那个高山岗，
言采其蝱。　　　　　　　　采些贝母慰忧伤。
女子善怀，　　　　　　　　女人虽然多想法，
亦各有行。　　　　　　　　各有理由和主张。

① 唁：吊问失国。
② 悠悠：路途遥远。
③ 嘉：好，赞同。
④ 臧：好。
⑤ 閟：闭塞，止息。

Patriotic Baroness Mu of Xu[1]

I gallop while I go
To share my brother's woe.
I ride down a long road
To my brother's abode.
The deputies will thwart
My plan and fret my heart.

"Although you say me nay,
I won't go back the other way.
Conservative are you
While farsight'd is my view?"

"Although you say me nay,
I won't stop on my way.
Conservative are you,
I can't accept your view."

I climb the sloping mound
To pick toad-lilies round.
Of woman don't make light!
My heart knows what is right.

[1] Baroness Mu of Xu, daughter of Duchess Xuan Jiang (See Poem "Scandals") of Wei, complained that the deputies of Xu did not allow her to go back to Wei to condole with her brother Duke Wen on the desolation of his State after the death of Duke Dai in 659 B.C., and to appeal to a mighty State on its behalf. It was contrary, however, to the rules of propriety for a lady in her position to return to her native State, so she picked toad-lilies which might, it was said, assuage her sorrow.

许人尤之，	许国大夫反对我，
众稚且狂。	真是幼稚又愚妄。
我行其野，	我正行走原野上，
芃芃①其麦。	麦苗油油长得旺。
控②于大邦，	奔告大国来帮忙，
谁因谁极。	靠着谁来救危亡。
大夫君子，	大夫君子众人们，
无我有尤。	不要再把我阻挡。
百尔所思，	你们纵有好计策，
不如我所之。	不如我去走一趟。

① 芃芃：草木茂盛的样子。
② 控：求告。

My countrymen put blame
On me and feel no shame.

I go across the plains;
Thick and green grow the grains.
I'll plead to mighty land,
Who'd hold out helping hand.
"Deputies, don't you see
The fault lies not with me?
Whatever may think you,
It's not so good as my view."

卫 风

淇 奥①

瞻彼淇奥，	看那淇水转弯处，
绿竹猗猗②。	绿竹婀娜真茂密。
有匪君子，	文雅风流美君子，
如切③如磋④，	如经切磋玉骨器，
如琢⑤如磨⑥。	雕琢玉石美如许。
瑟兮僩⑦兮，	庄严啊威武，
赫兮咺⑧兮。	威仪啊磊落。
有匪君子，	这个文雅的君子，
终不可谖⑨兮！	教人记住不能忘！

瞻彼淇奥，	看那淇水转弯处，
绿竹青青。	绿竹青青真茂密。
有匪君子，	文雅风流美君子，
充耳琇莹，	耳充宝石真晶莹，
会弁如星。	帽缝美玉如明星。

① 奥：弯曲处。
② 猗猗：长而美。
③ 切：治骨曰切。
④ 磋：治象牙曰磋。
⑤ 琢：治玉曰琢。
⑥ 磨：治石曰磨。
⑦ 僩（xiàn）：宽大、威武。
⑧ 咺（xuān）：威仪。
⑨ 谖：忘记。

Songs Collected in Wei, Modern Henan

Duke Wu of Wei[①]

Behold by riverside
Green bamboos in high glee.
Our duke is dignified
Like polished ivory
And stone or jade refined.
With solemn gravity
And elevated mind,
The duke we love a lot
Should never be forgot.

Behold by riverside
Bamboos with soft green shade.
Our duke is dignified
When crowned with strings of jade
As bright as stars we find.

---

① This song was written in praise of Duke Wu who ruled the State of Wei in 811—751 B. C. The duke cultivated the principles of government. The people increased in number, and others flocked to the State. In 770 B. C. when King You of Zhou was killed by a barbarian tribe, the duke led his army to the rescue of Zhou and rendered such great service against the enemy that King Ping appointed him a minister of the royal court.

瑟兮僩兮，	庄严啊威武，
赫兮咺兮。	威仪啊磊落。
有匪君子，	这个文雅的君子，
终不可谖兮！	教人记住不能忘！

瞻彼淇奥，	看那淇水转弯处，
绿竹如箦①。	绿竹郁郁真茂密。
有匪君子，	文雅风流美君子，
如金如锡，	才学精深如金锡，
如圭如璧。	品行洁美如圭璧。
宽兮绰兮，	宽厚啊温文啊，
猗重较②兮。	靠倚在车旁。
善戏谑兮，	谈笑风趣易接近，
不为虐兮。	不骄不躁不刻薄。

考③ 槃④

考槃在涧，	快乐啊溪水旁，
硕人之宽⑤。	贤人心舒畅。
独寐寤言，	独睡独醒独自说，
永矢弗谖。	这样的乐趣永不忘。

---

① 箦（zé）：密密层层的样子。
② 重较：古时车厢横木两端伸出的弯木。
③ 考：成就。
④ 槃：快乐。
⑤ 宽：放松。

With solemn gravity
And elevated mind,
The duke we love a lot
Should never be forgot.

Behold by riverside
Bamboos so lush and green.
Our duke is dignified
With gold-or tin-like sheen.
With his sceptre in hand,
He is in gentle mood;
By his chariot he'd stand;
At jesting he is good,
But he is never rude.

A Happy Hermit[①]

By riverside unknown
A hermit builds his cot.
He sleeps, wakes, speaks alone;
Such joy won't be forgot.

[①] It was said that this song was directed against Duke Zhuang of Wei, who did not walk in the footsteps of his father Duke Wu, and by his neglect of his duties led men of worth to withdraw from public lire into retirement.

考槃在阿，	快乐啊山窝里，
硕人之薖①。	贤人多惬意。
独寐②寤③歌，	独睡独醒独歌唱，
永矢弗过。	这样的乐趣永难忘。
考槃在陆，	快乐啊平地上，
硕人之轴④。	贤人在徜徉。
独寐寤宿，	独睡独醒独自卧，
永矢弗告。	这样的快乐不张扬。

硕　人

硕人其颀⑤，	有个美人身颀秀，
衣锦褧⑥衣。	锦衣外面布衣罩。
齐侯之子，	她是齐侯的女儿，
卫侯之妻，	卫侯的妻子，
东宫之妹，	太子的妹妹，
邢侯之姨，	邢侯的小姨子，
谭公维私⑦。	谭公是她的妹夫。

① 薖（guō）：快乐。
② 寐：睡觉。
③ 寤：醒来。
④ 轴：放心，舒畅。
⑤ 颀：身段修长而健美。
⑥ 褧（jiǒng）：罩袍，披风。
⑦ 私：古代女子称姊姐的丈夫曰私。

By mountainside unknown
A hermit will not fret.
He sleeps, Wakes, sings alone:
A joy never to forget.

On wooded land unknown
A hermit lives, behold!
He sleeps, wakes, dwells alone
A joy ne'er to be told.

The Duke's Bride[①]

The buxom lady's big and tall,
A cape o'er her robe of brocade.
Her father, brothers, husband all
Are dukes or marquis of high grade.
Like lard congealed her skin is tender,
Her fingers like soft blades of reed;
Like larva white her neck is slender,

---

① This was the first description of a beautiful lady in Chinese poetry. The beautiful lady was married to Duke Zhuang of Wei who reigned in 757—735 B. C. but she bore no children and brought up Duke Huan who was murdered by his half-brother in 718 B. C. (See Poem "A Farewell Song")

手如柔荑，	手指像茅草的嫩芽，
肤如凝脂，	皮肤像凝冻的白脂，
领如蝤蛴①，	脖颈像白而长的蝤蛴，
齿如瓠犀②，	牙齿像整齐的瓠瓜子，
螓③首蛾眉。	前额方正眉细弯。
巧笑倩兮，	轻巧笑时酒窝动，
美目盼兮。	四顾望时眼波转。
硕人敖敖，	有个美人身颀秀，
说④于农郊。	车子停歇在近郊。
四牡有骄，	四匹雄马气势骄，
朱幩⑤镳镳，	马勒绸带红绸飘，
翟茀⑥以朝。	雉羽蔽车来上朝。
大夫夙退，	大夫可以早退朝，
无使君劳。	不教君主多辛劳。
河水洋洋，	黄河流水浩洋洋，
北流活活，	向北流去哗哗响，
施罛⑦濊濊，	渔网撒向水中央，
鳣鲔发发，	鳣鱼鲔鱼全入网，

① 蝤蛴：天牛的幼虫，身体长而白。
② 瓠犀（hù xī）：葫芦籽，洁白而整齐。
③ 螓（qín）：像蝉而比蝉小的一种虫，额头方正。
④ 说：停止。
⑤ 朱幩（fén）：系在马衔两边用来装饰的红绸。
⑥ 翟茀（fú）：用山鸡毛装饰的车子。
⑦ 罛（gū）：渔网。

Her teeth like rows of melon-seed,
Her forehead like a dragonfly's,
Her arched brows curved like a bow.
Ah! Dark on white her speaking eyes,
Her cheeks with smiles and dimples glow,

The buxom lady goes along;
She passes outskirts to be wed.
Four steeds run vigorous and strong,
Their bits adorned with trappings red.
Her cab with pheasant-feathered screen
Proceeds to the court in array.
Retire, officials, from the scene!
Leave duke and her without delay!

The Yellow River wide and deep
Rolls northward its jubilant way.
When nets are played out, fishes leap
And splash and throw on reeds much spray.

葭菼① 揭揭②，　　　　　　　芦苇荻梗长正旺，
庶姜孽孽③，　　　　　　　从嫁的姜女盛妆忙，
庶士有朅④。　　　　　　　护送的武士气宇轩昂。

氓⑤

氓之蚩蚩⑥，　　　　　　　那人满脸笑嘻嘻，
抱布贸丝。　　　　　　　抱着布匹来换丝。
匪来贸丝，　　　　　　　不是真的来换丝，
来即我谋。　　　　　　　前来找我谈婚事。
送子涉淇，　　　　　　　送你渡过淇水去，
至于顿丘。　　　　　　　直到顿丘才分手。
匪我愆⑦期，　　　　　　　不是我要误婚期，
子无良媒。　　　　　　　是你没有请良媒。
将⑧子无怒，　　　　　　　求你不要生我气，
秋以为期。　　　　　　　清秋时节是佳期。

① 葭菼（tǎn）：荻苇。
② 揭揭：高高上扬的样子。
③ 孽孽：盛妆的样子。
④ 朅（qiè）：英武敏健的样子。
⑤ 氓：野民，村民。
⑥ 蚩蚩：憨厚嘻嘻的样子。
⑦ 愆：错过，失约。
⑧ 将：请。

Richly-dressed maids and warriors keep
Attendance on her bridal day.

A Faithless Man[1]

A man seemed free from guile;
In trade he wore a smile.
He'd barter cloth for thread;
No, to me he'd be wed.
I saw him cross the ford,
But gave him not my word.
I said by hillside green:
"You have no go-between.
Try to find one, I pray.
In autumn be the day."

---

[1] A woman who had been seduced into an improper connection, now cast off, related and bemoaned her sad case.

乘彼垝①垣，　　　　　　　登上坍坏残城墙，
以望复关。　　　　　　　眺望你在的复关。
不见复关，　　　　　　　没有看见那复关，
泣涕涟涟。　　　　　　　伤心落泪涕涟涟。
既见复关，　　　　　　　已经看到那复关，
载笑载言。　　　　　　　转眼就是笑开颜。
尔卜尔筮，　　　　　　　你已卜卦又请筮，
体无咎言②。　　　　　　还好没有不吉话。
以尔车来，　　　　　　　打发你车来一趟，
以我贿③迁。　　　　　　把我嫁妆一齐装。

桑之未落，　　　　　　　桑树叶儿还未落，
其叶沃若。　　　　　　　润泽繁盛又新鲜。
于嗟鸠兮，　　　　　　　小小斑鸠鸟儿啊，
无食桑葚。　　　　　　　不要去吃那桑葚儿！
于嗟女兮，　　　　　　　年纪青青姑娘啊，
无与士耽④。　　　　　　不要太爱男人啊！
士之耽兮，　　　　　　　男人若是爱恋深，
犹可说⑤也。　　　　　　可以停止以脱身。
女之耽兮，　　　　　　　姑娘若是恋爱深，
不可说也。　　　　　　　永无休止难脱身。

① 垝：毁坏。
② 咎言：不吉利的言辞。
③ 贿：财物，嫁妆。
④ 耽：沉湎。
⑤ 说：即"脱"，解脱。

I climbed the wall to wait
To see him pass the gate.
I did not see him pass;
My tears streamed down, alas!
When I saw him pass by,
I'd laugh with joy and cry.
Both reed and tortoise shell
Foretold all would be well.
"Come with your cart," I said,
"To you I will be wed."

How fresh were mulberries
With their fruit on the trees!
Beware, O turtledove,
Eat not the fruit of love!
It will intoxicate.
Do not repent too late!
Man may do what he will;
He can atone it still.
No one will e'er condone
The wrong a woman's done.

桑之落矣，　　　　　　桑树叶儿落下来，
其黄而陨。　　　　　　干黄憔悴掉下来。
自我徂尔，　　　　　　自从来到你们家，
三岁食贫。　　　　　　三年贫困度苦寒。
淇水汤汤，　　　　　　淇水浩浩又荡荡，
渐车帷裳。　　　　　　湿了一半车帷帐。
女也不爽①，　　　　　我的感情没变样，
士贰②其行。　　　　　你的行为不一样。
士也罔极③，　　　　　男人心思不可猜，
二三其德。　　　　　　三心二意无德行。

三岁为妇，　　　　　　三年媳妇不算短，
靡室劳矣，　　　　　　全家活儿一人担。
夙兴夜寐，　　　　　　早起晚睡已习惯，
靡有朝矣。　　　　　　日日夜夜忙不完。
言既遂④矣，　　　　　生活渐渐顺了心，
至于暴矣。　　　　　　脾气慢慢成暴残。
兄弟不知，　　　　　　兄弟不知这些事，
咥⑤其笑矣。　　　　　看见我时展笑颜。
静言思之，　　　　　　细细想想这些事，
躬自悼矣。　　　　　　只能一人独伤怨。

① 爽：差错，过失。
② 贰：前后言行不一。
③ 极：准则。
④ 遂：安定，顺心。
⑤ 咥：带有讥讽的笑。

The mulberries appear
With yellow leaves and sear.
E'er since he married me,
I've shared his poverty.
Deserted, from him I part;
The flood has wet my cart.
I have done nothing wrong;
He changes all along.
He's fickle to excess,
Capricious, pitiless.

Three years I was his wife
And led a toilsome life.
Each day I early rose
And late I sought repose.
But he found fault with me
And treated me cruelly.
My brothers who didn't know
Let their jeers at me go.
Mutely I ruminate
And I deplore my fate.

及尔偕老，	原想和你同到老，
老使我怨。	现实让我心满怨。
淇则有岸，	淇水宽宽也有岸，
隰①则有泮②。	漯河阔阔也有边。
总角③之宴，	记得童年多欢乐，
言笑晏晏④。	说说笑笑无愁烦。
信誓旦旦，	山盟海誓两相愿，
不思其反⑤。	回忆这些是枉然。
反是不思，	别想从前多喜欢，
亦已焉哉！	一切不再是从前！

竹 竿

籊籊⑥竹竿，	钓鱼竹竿细又长，
以钓于淇。	当年垂钓淇水上。
岂不尔思？	难道旧游不曾想？
远莫致之。	道路遥远难回乡。
泉源在左，	泉水源头在左边，
淇水在右。	淇河流水向右边。
女子有行，	姑娘自从出嫁后，
远兄弟父母。	远离父母兄弟前。

① 隰：水名，又称漯河。
② 泮：岸。
③ 总角：小孩子的发型，指童年。
④ 晏晏：融洽，快乐。
⑤ 反：反复，变心。
⑥ 籊籊（tì tì）：长而细的样子。

I'd live with him till old;
My grief was not foretold.
The endless stream has shores;
My endless grief e'er pours.
When we were girl and boy,
We'd talk and laugh with joy.
He pledged to me his troth.
Could he forget his oath?
He's forgot what he swore.
Should I say any more?

A Lovesick Fisherman[①]

With long rod of bamboo
I fish in River Qi.
Home, how I long for you,
Far-off a thousand li!

At left the Spring flows on;
At right the River clear.
To wed they saw me gone,
Leaving my parents dear.

---

① A daughter of the House of Wei, married in another state, expressed her longing to revisit the scenes of her youth, where she had rambled in elegant dress between River Qi and the Spring. It was said that the daughter was Baroness Mu of Xu (See Poem "Patriotic Baroness Mu of Xu").

淇水在右。　　　　　　　　淇河流水向右边，
泉源在左。　　　　　　　　泉水源头在左边。
巧笑之瑳①，　　　　　　　巧妙笑时齿鲜白，
佩玉之傩②。　　　　　　　佩玉摇动声连连。

淇水滺滺，　　　　　　　　淇水流长悠悠流，
桧楫松舟。　　　　　　　　桧树做楫松做舟。
驾言出游，　　　　　　　　只好驾车来出游，
以写我忧。　　　　　　　　聊以解除我心忧。

芄 兰

芄兰之支，　　　　　　　　芄兰的枝，
童子佩觿③。　　　　　　　童子佩戴象牙锥。
虽则佩觿，　　　　　　　　虽然佩戴象牙锥，
能不我知。　　　　　　　　才能低下我知道。
容④兮遂兮，　　　　　　　摇摇摆摆装得像，
垂带悸⑤兮。　　　　　　　带子似的下垂样。

芄兰之叶，　　　　　　　　芄兰的叶，
童子佩韘⑥。　　　　　　　童子佩戴象牙玦。

① 瑳：玉色鲜白。
② 傩：有节奏。
③ 觿（xī）：用象骨制作，形状如锥的解结用具。
④ 容：形式像。
⑤ 悸：带子下垂的样子。
⑥ 韘（shè）：用象骨制作的射箭用具，戴于右手拇指上，俗称扳指。

The River clear at right,
At left the Spring flows on.
O my smiles beaming bright
And ringing gems are gone!

The long, long River flows
With boats of pine home-bound.
My boat along it goes.
O let my grief be drowned!

A Widow in Love[①]

The creeper's pods hang like
The young man's girdle spike.
An adult's spike he wears;
For us he no longer cares.
He puts on airs and swings
To and fro tassel-strings.

The creeper's leaves also swing;
The youth wears archer's ring.

---

① It was said that the conceited youth alluded to Duke Hui of Wei who murdered his elder brother and succeeded to the State in 718 B. C. (See Poem "A Farewell Song")

虽则佩韘,	虽然佩戴象牙玦,
能不我甲。	才能不把我超越。
容兮遂兮,	摇摇摆摆装得像,
垂带悸兮。	带子似的下垂样。

河 广

谁谓河广?	谁说黄河太宽广?
一苇杭之。	一束芦苇可以航。
谁谓宋远?	谁说宋国太遥远?
跂①予望之。	踮起脚来可以望。

谁谓河广?	谁说黄河太宽广?
曾不容刀。	难容一只小船荡。
谁谓宋远?	谁说宋国太遥远?
曾不崇朝②。	走到宋国一早上。

伯③兮

伯兮朅④兮,	夫君啊,多英武,
邦之桀兮。	是国家的英雄。

① 跂:踮起脚尖。
② 崇朝:整个早上。
③ 伯:周代妇女称丈夫为伯。
④ 朅(qiè):威武健壮。

An archer's ring he wears;
For us he no longer cares.
He puts on airs and swings
To and fro tassel-strings.

The River Wide[①]

Who says the River's wide?
A reed could reach the other side.
Who says Song's far-off? Lo!
I could see it on tiptoe.

Who says the River's wide?
A boat could reach the other side.
Who says Song's far away?
I could reach it within a day.

My Lord[②]

My lord is brave and bright,
A hero in our land,

---

① This song was said to be written by a daughter of Xuan Jiang who longed to see her son, Duke Xiang of Song.
② A wife mourned over the protracted absence of her lord on the King's service around 706 B.C. This was considered as the earliest song of a wife longing for her husband in service.

伯也执殳①，	夫君拿着殳杖，
为王前驱。	为君王当先锋。
自伯之东，	自从夫君走向东，
首如飞蓬。	我的头发乱蓬蓬。
岂无膏沐②，	难道没有脂和油，
谁适为容？	为谁打扮为谁容？
其雨其雨，	总是觉得该下雨，
杲杲③出日。	一轮太阳高高挂。
愿言思伯，	一心只把夫君想，
甘心首疾。	想得心疼头也痛。
焉得谖④草？	哪儿去找忘忧草，
言树⑤之背⑥。	把它栽到北堂好。
愿言思伯，	一心只把夫君想，
使我心痗⑦。	病驻心头忘不了。

① 殳（shū）：古代的一种兵器。
② 膏沐：化妆用的油脂。
③ 杲杲（gǎo gǎo）：太阳出来火红光亮的样子。
④ 谖（xuān）草：忘忧草。
⑤ 树：栽种。
⑥ 背：北堂。
⑦ 痗（mèi）：病痛。

A vanguard in King's fight,
With a lance in his hand.

Since my lord eastward went,
Like thistle looks my hair.
Have I no anointment?
For whom should I look fair?

Let it rain, let it rain!
The sun shines bright instead.
I miss my lord in vain,
Heedless of aching head.

Where's the Herb to Forget?
To plant it north I'd start.
Missing my lord, I fret:
It makes me sick at heart.

有 狐

有狐绥绥[1]，	有只狐狸独自走，
在彼淇梁。	在那淇水桥头上。
心之忧矣，	我的心里直发愁，
之子无裳。	这人裙裳也没有。
有狐绥绥，	有只狐狸缓缓走，
在彼淇厉[2]。	在那淇水摆渡口。
心之忧矣，	我的心里直发愁，
之子无带。	这人衣带也没有。
有狐绥绥，	有只狐狸慢慢走，
在彼淇侧。	在那淇水旁边头。
心之忧矣，	我的心里直发愁，
之子无服。	这人衣衫也没有。

木 瓜

投[3]我以木瓜，	姑娘送我木瓜，
报之以琼琚[4]。	我用琼琚报答她。
匪报也，	琼琚哪能报答，
永以为好也。	是想永远相好啊。

[1] 绥绥：慢慢独自行走。
[2] 厉：水深处的渡口。
[3] 投：男女互相投赠东西，是民间一种求爱的方式。
[4] 琼琚、琼瑶、琼玖：美玉。

A Lonely Husband[①]

Like lonely fox he goes
On the bridge over there.
My heart sad and drear grows:
He has no underwear.

Like lonely fox he goes
At the ford over there.
My heart sad and drear grows:
He has no belt to wear.

Like lonely fox he goes
By riverside o'er there.
My heart sad and drear grows:
He has no dress whate'er.

Gifts[②]

She throws a quince to me;
I give her a green jade
Not in return, you see,
But to show acquaintance made.

[①] It was said that in this song a woman expressed her desire for a husband, for through the misery and desolation of the State of Wei, many, both men and women, were left unmarried or had lost their partners.
[②] This song referred to an interchange of courtesies between a lover and his mistress.

投我以木桃，　　　　　　姑娘送我红桃，
报之以琼瑶。　　　　　　我用琼瑶报答她。
匪报也，　　　　　　　　琼瑶哪能报答，
永以为好也。　　　　　　是想永远相好啊。

投我以木李，　　　　　　姑娘送我木李，
报之以琼玖。　　　　　　我用琼玖报答她。
匪报也，　　　　　　　　琼玖哪能报答，
永以为好也。　　　　　　是想永远相好啊。

She throws a peach to me;
I give her a white jade
Not in return, you see,
But to show friendship made.

She throws a plum to me;
I give her jasper fair
Not in return, you see,
But to show love fore'er.

王　风

黍　离

彼黍离离①,	看那黍子成行盛茂,
彼稷之苗。	看那高粱正发新苗。
行迈靡靡②,	就要远行难迈步,
中心摇摇③。	无限忧愁在心头。
知我者谓我心忧,	知道我的人说我心里烦忧,
不知我者谓我何求。	不知道我的人说我有什么要求。
悠悠苍天,	遥远的苍天啊,
此何人哉!	这是谁造成的啊!
彼黍离离,	看那黍子成行盛茂,
彼稷之穗。	看那高粱正抽早穗。
行迈靡靡,	就要远行难迈步,
中心如醉。	心中恍惚如醉酒。
知我者谓我心忧,	知道我的人说我心里烦忧,
不知我者谓我何求。	不知道我的人说我有什么要求。

---

① 离离：长得一行一行茂盛的样子。
② 靡靡：行走迟缓的样子。
③ 摇摇：心神不安，忧伤的样子。

Songs Collected around the Capital, Modern Henan

The Ruined Capital[①]

The millet drops its head;
The sorghum is in sprout.
Slowly I trudge and tread;
My heart is tossed about.
Those who know me will say
My heart is sad and bleak;
Those who don't know me may
Ask me for what I seek.
O boundless azure sky,
Who's ruined the land and why?

The millet drops its head;
The sorghum in the ear.
Slowly I trudge and tread;
My heart seems drunk and drear
Those who know me will say
My heart is sad and bleak;

---

① In 769 B. C. King Ping of the Zhou dynasty removed the capital to the east and from this time the kings of Zhou sank nearly to the level of the princes of the States. An official seeing the desolation of the old capital wrote this song expressing his melancholy.

悠悠苍天，　　　　　　　遥远的苍天啊，
此何人哉！　　　　　　　这是谁造成的啊！

彼黍离离，　　　　　　　看那黍子成行盛茂，
彼稷之实。　　　　　　　看那高粱正在结实。
行迈靡靡，　　　　　　　就要远行难迈步，
中心如噎①。　　　　　　心口如噎真难受。
知我者谓我心忧，　　　　知道我的人说我心里烦忧，
不知我者谓我何求。　　　不知道我的人说我
悠悠苍天，　　　　　　　有什么要求。
此何人哉！　　　　　　　遥远的苍天啊，
　　　　　　　　　　　　这是谁造成的啊！

君子于役②

君子于役，　　　　　　　夫君在服劳役，
不知其期，　　　　　　　不知他的归期。
曷至③哉？　　　　　　　什么时候回来？
鸡栖于埘④，　　　　　　鸡已纷纷飞上窝，

---

① 噎：气阻不顺。
② 役：服劳役。
③ 至：回家。
④ 埘（shí）：鸡窝。

Those who don't know me may
Ask me for what I seek.
O boundless azure sky,
Who's ruined the land and why?

The millet drops its head;
The sorghum is in grain.
Slowly I trudge and tread;
My heart seems choked with pain.
Those who know me will say
My heart is sad and bleak;
Those who don't know me may
Ask me for what I seek.
O boundless azure sky,
Who's ruined the land and why?

My Man Is Away[①]

My man's away to serve the State;
I can't anticipate
How long he will there stay
Or when he'll be on homeward way.

---

① This song expressed the feeling of a wife on the prolonged absence of her husband on service and her longing for his return.

日之夕矣，	太阳也已下山了，
羊牛下来。	牛羊纷纷下山岗。

君子于役，	夫君在服劳役，
如之何勿思！	怎么能够不想他！
君子于役，	夫君在服劳役，
不日不月。	没有准期要回来。

曷其有佸①？	什么时候能团圆？
鸡栖于桀②，	鸡已纷纷歇木桩，
日之夕矣，	太阳也下山了，
羊牛下括③。	牛羊纷纷下山坡。
君子于役，	夫君在服劳役，
苟无饥渴。	但愿不要饿肚肠。

君子阳阳 ④

君子阳阳，	君子走来喜洋洋，
左执簧，	左手拿着笙簧，

---

① 佸（huó）：会和，团圆。
② 桀：木桩。
③ 括：到来。
④ 阳阳：快乐。

The sun is setting in the west;
The fowls are roosting in their nest;

The sheep and cattle come to rest.
To serve the State my man's away.
How can I not think of him night and day?

My man's away to serve the state;
I can't anticipate
When we'll again have met.
The sun's already set;
The fowls are roosting in their nest;
The sheep and cattle come to rest.
To serve the state my man's away.
Keep him from hunger and thirst, I pray.

What Joy[①]

My man sings with delight;
In his left hand a flute of reed,

[①] It was said that this song showed the husband's satisfaction and his wife's joy on his return.

右招我由房^①。　　　　　　右手招我去游逛。
其乐只且!　　　　　　　　　快乐心花放!

君子陶陶^②,　　　　　　　君子走来乐陶陶,
左执翿^③,　　　　　　　　左手拿着羽旄扬,
右招我由敖。　　　　　　　右手招我去游遨。
其乐只且!　　　　　　　　　快乐心花放!

扬^④ 之水

扬之水,　　　　　　　　　　激扬的河水啊,
不流束薪。　　　　　　　　成捆的柴草漂不走。
彼其之子,　　　　　　　　那个人啊,
不与我戍^⑤申。　　　　　不和我去驻申地。
怀哉怀哉,　　　　　　　　想念啊想念!
曷月予还归哉?　　　　　　哪月我才能回去啊?

扬之水,　　　　　　　　　　激扬的河水啊,
不流束楚。　　　　　　　　成捆的荆条漂不走。
彼其之子,　　　　　　　　那个人啊,
不与我戍甫。　　　　　　　不和我去驻甫地。
怀哉怀哉,　　　　　　　　想念啊想念!

---

① 由房: 游戏玩耍。
② 陶陶: 和乐。
③ 翿(dào): 羽毛做的舞具。
④ 扬: 水流激荡。
⑤ 戍: 驻防。

He calls me to sing with his right,
What joy indeed!

My man dances in delight;
In his left hand a feather-screen,
He calls me to dance with his right.
What joy foreseen!

In Garrison[①]

Slowly the water flows;
Firewood can't be carried away.
You're afraid of your foes;
Why don't you in garrison stay?
How much for home I yearn!
O when may I return?

Slowly the water flows;
No thorn can be carried away.
You're afraid of your foes;
Why don't you in army camps stay?
How much for home I yearn!

---

① The troops of Zhou murmured against the lords who kept them on duty in the State of Shen, modern Nanyang. The water which flows so slowly and whose power is too weak to carry away firewood or thorn or rushes may allude to the Kingdom of Zhou, too weak to defend its frontiers.

曷月予还归哉？	哪月我才能回去啊？

扬之水，	激扬的河水啊，
不流束蒲。	成捆的蒲草漂不走。
彼其之子，	那个人啊，
不与我戍许。	不和我去驻许地。
怀哉怀哉，	想念啊想念！
曷月予还归哉？	哪月我才能回去啊？

中谷有蓷①

中谷有蓷，	谷中长着益母草，
暵②其干矣。	枝干枯槁将折断。
有女仳③离，	离弃之女伤心肝，
嘅④其叹矣。	感慨伤心又长叹。
嘅其叹矣，	感慨伤心又长叹，
遇人之艰难矣！	嫁个贤人可真难！

中谷有蓷，	谷中长着益母草，
暵其脩⑤矣。	蔫萎枯槁将发烂。
有女仳离，	离弃之女伤心肝，
条其歗⑥矣。	伤心不禁长声叹。

① 蓷（tuī）：益母草。
② 暵（hàn）：干枯。
③ 仳（pǐ）：离弃。
④ 嘅：叹息。
⑤ 脩：干肉，代指干。
⑥ 歗（xiào）：痛声。

O when may I return?

Slowly the water flows;
Rushes can't be carried away.
You're afraid of your foes;
Why don't you in army tents stay?
How much for home I yearn?
O when may I return?

Grief of a Deserted Wife[①]

Amid the vale grow mother-worts;
They are withered and dry.
There's a woman her lord deserts.
O hear her sigh!
O hear her sigh!
Her lord's a faithless guy.

Amid the vale grow mother-worts;
They are scorched and dry.
There's a woman her lord deserts.
O hear her cry!

---

① This song was expressive of pity for a deserted wife.

条其歗矣,　　　　　　　　　伤心不禁长声叹,
遇人之不淑矣!　　　　　　　嫁个男人是祸患!

中谷有蓷,　　　　　　　　　谷中长着益母草,
暵其湿矣。　　　　　　　　　根枝枯槁将朽坏。
有女仳离,　　　　　　　　　离弃之女伤心肝,
啜其泣矣。　　　　　　　　　伤心呜咽尽泣哭。
啜其泣矣,　　　　　　　　　伤心呜咽尽泣哭,
何嗟及矣!　　　　　　　　　后悔莫及空长叹!

兔　爰

有兔爰爰[①],　　　　　　　兔子自由自在,
雉离[②]于罗。　　　　　　　野鸡落入网来。
我生之初,　　　　　　　　　在我幼年生活时,
尚无为。　　　　　　　　　　尚无繁重劳役忙。
我生之后,　　　　　　　　　我生活一段时日后,
逢此百罹。　　　　　　　　　遭逢千百种灾殃。
尚寐,　　　　　　　　　　　还是睡觉吧,
无吪[③]!　　　　　　　　　 不动不声张!

有兔爰爰,　　　　　　　　　兔子自由自在,
雉离于罦[④]。　　　　　　　野鸡触入网中。

① 爰爰:自由自在行走的样子。
② 离:罹难,落入网中。
③ 吪:说话。
④ 罦:网。

O hear her cry!
She has met a bad guy.

Amid the vale grow mother-worts;
They are now drowned and wet.
There's a woman her lord deserts.
See her tears jet!
See her tears jet!
It's too late to regret.

Past and Present[1]

The rabbit runs away,
The pheasant in the net.
In my earliest day
For nothig did I fret;
In later years of care
All evils have I met.
O I would sleep fore'er.

The rabbit runs away,
The pheasant in the snare.

---

[1] The present referred to the time of King Ping (718—696 B. C.). The rabbit was said to be of a crafty nature while the pheasant to be bold and determined and easily snared.

我生之初，	在我幼年生活时，
尚无造①。	尚无荡役重繁忙。
我生之后，	我生活一段时日后，
逢此百忧。	遭逢千百种愁伤。
尚寐，	还是睡觉吧，
无觉！	不桓无声响！

有兔爰爰，	兔子自由自在，
雉离于罿②。	野鸡陷入网中。
我生之初，	在我幼年生活时，
尚无庸③。	尚无辛苦奔忙。
我生之后，	我生活一段时日后，
逢此百凶。	遭逢千百种凶险。
尚寐，	还是睡觉吧，
无聪！	不听犹死状！

葛藟

绵绵葛藟，	长长的野葛茎，
在河之浒。	在河边上生。
终远兄弟，	离别兄弟们，
谓他人父。	称呼他人为父。
谓他人父，	称呼他人为父，
亦莫我顾！	也没有人照顾我！

① 造：造作。
② 罿（tóng）：网。
③ 庸：劳役。

In my earliest day
For nothing did I care;
In later years of ache
I'm in grief and despair.
I'd sleep and never wake.

The rabbit runs away,
The pheasant in the trap.
In my earliest day
I lived without mishap;
But in my later year
All miseries appear.
I'd sleep and never hear.

A Refugee[①]

Creepers spread all the way
Along the river clear.
From brothers far away,
I call a stranger "father dear."
Though called "dear father," he
Seems not to care for me.

[①] A refugee mourned over his lot, unpitied by man and woman, old and young. The growth of creepers on the soil proper to them was presented by the refugee in contrast to his own position, torn from his family and proper soil.

绵绵葛藟,	长长的野葛茎,
在河之涘。	在河边上生。
终远兄弟,	离别兄弟们,
谓他人母。	称呼他人为娘。
谓他人母,	称呼他人为娘,
亦莫我有!	也没有人亲近我!

绵绵葛藟,	长长的野葛茎,
在河之漘①。	在河边上生。
终远兄弟,	离别兄弟们,
谓他人昆②。	称呼他人为兄。
谓他人昆,	称呼他人为兄,
亦莫我闻!	也没有人怜悯我!

采 葛

彼采葛兮,	那人正在采葛啊。
一日不见,	一天不见她,
如三月兮。	好像过去三个月。

彼采萧③兮,	那人正在采青蒿啊。
一日不见,	一天不见她,
如三秋④兮。	好像过去九个月。

① 漘(chún):同浒、涘,水边。
② 昆:兄长。
③ 萧:青蒿。
④ 秋:一个秋天三个月。三秋即九个月。

Creepers spread all the way
Beside the river clear.
From brothers far away,
I call a stranger "mother dear."
Though called "dear mother," she
Seems not to cherish me.

Creepers spread all the way
Beyond the river clear.
From brothers far away,
I call a stranger "brother dear."
Though called "dear Brother," he
Seems not to pity me.

One Day When I See Her Not[①]

To gather vine goes she.
I miss her whom I do not see,
One day seems longer than months three.

To gather reed goed she.
I miss her whom I do not see,
One day seems long as seasons three.

---

① It has become proverbial that a short absence from the lover seems to e long, and longer the more she is dwelt upon.

彼采艾兮，	那人正在采艾啊。
一日不见，	一天不见她，
如三岁兮。	好像过去了三年。

大 车

大车槛槛①，	大车经过声槛槛，
毳②衣如菼③。	车氊有似芦苇花。
岂不尔思，	难道是我不想你？
畏子不敢。	怕你犹豫心不敢。

大车啍啍④，	大车驶过慢吞吞，
毳衣如璊⑤。	车氊有似红玉色。
岂不尔思，	难道是我不想你？
畏子不奔。	怕你犹豫不相奔。

榖⑥则异室，	活着不能住一起，
死则同穴。	死去同埋一个圹。
谓予不信，	别不相信我的话，
有如皦⑦日。	青天太阳来做证。

① 槛槛：车行走的声音。
② 毳（cuì）：车上蔽风雨的毡子。
③ 菼（tǎn）：初生的芦苇花。
④ 啍啍：车缓慢而笨重的声音。
⑤ 璊（mén）：赤色的玉。
⑥ 榖：活着。
⑦ 皦（jiǎo）：光明。

To gather herbs goes she.
I miss her whom I do not see,
One day seems longer than years three.

To Her Captive Lord [1]

Rumbling your cart,
Reedlike your gown,
I miss you in my heart.
How dare I make it known?

Rattling your cart,
Reddish your gown,
I miss you in my heart.
How dare I have it shown?

Living, we dwell apart;
Dead, the same grave we'll share.
Am I not true at heart?
By the bright sun I swear.

---

[1] This song was said to be written by the beautiful Lady of Peach Blossom, whose lord became a captive of the prince of Chu.

丘中有麻

丘中有麻,　　　　　　　　土丘上面种苎麻,
彼留子嗟。　　　　　　　　住在留地的名子嗟。
彼留子嗟,　　　　　　　　住在留地的名子嗟,
将①其来施②。　　　　　　愿他高兴走来吧。

丘中有麦,　　　　　　　　土丘上面种大麦,
彼留子国。　　　　　　　　住在留地的名子国。
彼留子国,　　　　　　　　住在留地的名子国,
将其来食。　　　　　　　　愿他快快来进食。

丘中有李,　　　　　　　　土丘上面种李树,
彼留之子。　　　　　　　　居住留地的好儿郎。
彼留之子,　　　　　　　　居住留地的好儿郎,
贻我佩玖。　　　　　　　　送我美玉永难忘。

① 将：请愿。
② 施：高兴的样子。

To Her Lover[①]

Hemp on the mound I see.
Who's there detaining thee?
Who's there detaining thee?
From coming jauntily to me?

Wheat on the mound I'm thinking of.
Who detains thee above?
Who detains thee above
From coming with me to make love?

On the mound stands plum tree.
Who's there detaining thee?
Who's there detaining thee
From giving girdle gems to me?

---

① A woman longed for the presence of her lover who, she thought, was detained from her by another woman.

郑 风

缁^① 衣

缁衣之宜兮，　　　　　　　黑衣正合适啊，
敝予又改为兮。　　　　　　破了我又替你改制。
适子之馆^②兮，　　　　　到你的官舍里啊，
还予授子之粲兮。　　　　　回来我给你备食饭。

缁衣之好兮，　　　　　　　黑衣真美好啊，
敝予又改造兮。　　　　　　破了我又替你改造。
适子之馆兮，　　　　　　　到你的客馆里啊，
还予授子之粲兮。　　　　　回来我给你备食馔。

缁衣之席^③兮，　　　　　黑衣真宽大啊，
敝予又改作兮。　　　　　　破了我又替你改做。
适子之馆兮，　　　　　　　到你的官舍里啊，
还予授子之粲兮。　　　　　回来我给你备佳饭。

① 缁：黑色。
② 馆：客舍。
③ 席：宽大。

Songs Collected in Zheng, Modern Henan

A Good Wife[1]

The black-dyed robe befits you well;
When it's worn out, I'll make another new.
You go to work in your hotel;
Come back, I'll make a meal for you.

The black-dyed robe becomes you well;
When it's worn out, I'll get another new.
You go to work in your hotel;
Come back, I'll make a meal for you.

The black-dyed robe does suit you well;
When it's worn out, you'll have another new.
You go to work in your hotel;
Come back, I'll make a meal foryou.

---

[1] It was said that this song was expressive of the wife's regard that was due to the virtue and ability of her lord.

将① 仲子

将仲子兮，	请求仲子啊，
无逾我里，	不要翻入我闾里，
无折我树杞。	不要攀折我家的杞。
岂敢爱之？	难道我是爱惜它？
畏我父母。	只怕我父母要说话。
仲可怀也，	仲子叫我牵挂，
父母之言，	可是父母的话，
亦可畏也。	也让我有些害怕。

将仲子兮，	请求仲子啊，
无逾我墙，	不要跨过我院墙，
无折我树桑。	不要攀折我家的桑。
岂敢爱之？	难道我是爱惜它？
畏我诸兄。	只怕我兄长要说话。
仲可怀也，	仲子叫我牵挂，
诸兄之言，	可是兄长的话，
亦可畏也。	也让我有些害怕。

将仲子兮，	请求仲子啊，
无逾我园，	不要翻进我后园，
无折我树檀。	不要攀折我家的檀。
岂敢爱之？	难道我是爱惜它？
畏人之多言。	只怕我邻居要说话。

① 将（qiāng）：请求。

Cadet My Dear[1]

Cadet my dear,
Don't leap into my hamlet, please,
Nor break my willow trees!
Not that I care for these;
It is my parents that I fear.
Much as I love you, dear,
How can I not be afraid
Of what my parents might have said!

Cadet my dear,
Don't leap over my wall, please,
Nor break my mulberries!
Not that I care for these;
It is my brothers that I fear.
Much as I love you, dear,
How can I not be afraid
Of what my brothers might have said!

Cadet my dear,
Don't leap into my garden, please,
Nor break my sandal trees!
Not that I care for these;
It is my neighbors that I fear.

---

[1] A woman begged her lover not to excite the suspicions and remarks of her parents and others.

仲可怀也,	仲子叫我牵挂,
人之多言,	可是邻居的话,
亦可畏也。	也让我有些害怕。

叔于田[1]

叔于田,	叔在打猎,
巷无居人。	大街小巷没有人。
岂无居人?	街巷怎会无人?
不如叔也,	谁都不如叔啊,
洵美且仁。	那么美好又慈仁!

叔于狩[2],	叔在冬天打猎,
巷无饮酒。	街巷没有人喝酒。
岂无饮酒?	街巷怎会无人喝酒?
不如叔也,	谁都不如叔啊,
洵美且好。	那么良善又清秀!

叔适野,	叔在郊外打猎,
巷无服马[3]。	街巷没有人驾马。
岂无服马?	街巷怎么会无人驾马?
不如叔也,	谁都不如叔啊,
洵美且武。	那么俊美又英武!

[1] 田:打猎。
[2] 狩:冬天打猎。
[3] 服马:用马驾车。

Much as I love you, dear,
How can I not be afraid
of what my neighbors might have said!

The Young Cadet[①]

The young cadet to chase hasgone;
It seems there's no man in thetown.
Is it true there's none in the town?
It's only that I cannot find
Another hunter so handsome andkind.

The young cadet's gone hunting in the wood.
In the town there's no drinker good.
Is it true there's no drinker good?
In the town no drinker of wine
Looks so handsome and fine.

The young cadet has gone to countryside;
In the town there's none who can ride.
Is it true there's none who can ride?
I cannot find among the young and old
Another rider so handsome and bold.

---

① It was said that the young cadet referred to the younger brother of Duke Zhuang of Zheng who succeeded Duke Wu in 742 B. C.

大叔于田

叔于田,	大叔在打猎,
乘乘①马。	四匹马儿拉着车。
执辔②如组,	手握缰绳如丝带,
两骖③如舞。	两匹边马像舞蹈。
叔在薮④,	叔在泽地草边,
火烈具举。	几处猎火齐烧。
袒裼⑤暴虎⑥,	赤膊空拳捉猛虎,
献于公所。	献给公爵去。
将⑦叔无狃⑧,	请叔不要再这样,
戒其伤女。	小心它会伤害你。
叔于田,	大叔在打猎,
乘乘黄。	四匹黄马拉着车儿。
两服上襄,	中间两马并驾前,
两骖雁行。	外面边马如雁行。
叔在薮,	叔在湖地草边,
火烈具扬。	一片猎火高扬。

① 乘乘（chéng shèng）马：乘坐四匹马拉的车。前乘字指乘坐，后乘字指四匹马拉的车。
② 辔：马缰绳。
③ 骖：四匹马中外面的两匹马。
④ 薮：沼泽丛林。
⑤ 袒裼（tǎn xī）：赤膊。
⑥ 暴虎：空手打虎。
⑦ 将：请。
⑧ 无狃（niǔ）：不要习以为常，不在意。

Hunting[①]

Our lord goes hunting in the land,
Mounted in his cab with four steeds.
He waves and weaves the reins in hand;
Two outside horses dance with speed.
Our lord goes hunting in grass land;
The hunters' torches flame in a ring.
He seizes a tiger with bared hand
And then presents it to the king.
Don't try, my lord, to do it again
For fear you may get hurt with pain!

Mounted in his chariot and four,
Hunting afield our lord does go.
The inside horses run before;
Two on the outside follow in a row.
Our lord goes to the waterside;
The hunters' torches blaze up high.

---

① This was the earliest description of hunting in Chinese poetry.

叔善射忌,	叔是射箭神手,
又良御忌。	赶车技术高超。
抑磬控忌,	一会儿勒马不进,
抑纵送①忌。	一会儿马蹄奔放。

叔于田,	大叔在打猎,
乘乘鸨②。	四匹花马拉着车儿。
两服齐首,	中间两马齐并头,
两骖如手。	外面边马如两手。
叔在薮,	叔在湖地草边,
火烈具阜③。	一片猎火高照。
叔马慢忌,	叔的马儿慢悠闲,
叔发罕忌。	叔的弓箭发得少。
抑释掤④忌,	把箭放在箭袋里,
抑鬯⑤弓忌。	把弓放在弓袋里。

清 人

清人在彭,	清地的兵驻彭地,
驷介⑥旁旁⑦。	四马披甲真强壮。

---

① 纵送：一面射箭，一面追赶野兽。
② 鸨（bǎo）：毛色黑白相杂的马。
③ 阜：旺盛。
④ 掤（bīng）：箭筒盖子。
⑤ 鬯（chàng）：装弓的袋子。
⑥ 驷介：四匹马披甲驾车。
⑦ 旁旁：强盛的样子。

He knows not only how to ride
But also shoot with his sharp eye.
He runs and stops his steeds at will
And shoots his arrows with great skill.

Mounted in cab and four steeds fine,
Our lord goes hunting in the lands.
Two on the inside have their heads in a line;
Two on the outside follow like two hands.
To waterside our lord does go;
The hunters' fire spreads everywhere.
His grey and yellow steeds go slow;
The arrows he shoots become rare.
Aside his quiver now he lays
And returns his bow to the case.

Qing Warriors[①]

Qing warriors stationed out,
Four mailed steeds run about.

---

① This was a satire against Duke Wen who ruled in the State of Zheng(662—627 B. C.) but manoeuvred uselessly an army of Qing on the frontier.

二矛重英，	两矛饰着重缨络，
河上乎翱翔。	河边闲游又翱翔。

清人在消，	清地的兵驻消地，
驷介麃麃①。	四马披甲雄骁骁。
二矛重乔②，	两矛披着野鸡毛，
河上乎逍遥。	河边闲游多逍遥。

清人在轴，	清地的兵驻轴地，
驷介陶陶。	四马披甲如风跑。
左旋右抽，	车子左转右抽刀，
中军③作好。	将军武姿真是好。

羔 裘

羔裘如濡④，	羊羔皮袍光又润，
洵直且侯⑤。	真是舒直又美好。
彼其之子，	那个人啊，
舍命不渝。	舍弃性命不改变。

羔裘豹饰，	羊羔皮袍饰豹皮，
孔武有力。	显得英武又有力。

① 麃麃（biāo biāo）：威武的样子。
② 乔：野鸡毛。
③ 中军：军中的统帅。
④ 濡：湿滑润泽。
⑤ 侯：美好。

Two spears adorned with feathers red,
Along the stream they roam ahead.

Qing warriors stationed on the shore
Look martial in their cab and four.
Two spears with pheasant's feathers red,
Along the stream they stroll ahead.

Qing warriors stationed on the stream
Look proud in their cab and mailed team.
Driver at left, spearsman at right,
The general shows his great delight.

Officer in Lamb's Fur[①]

His fur of lamb is white
As the man is upright.
The officer arises
Unchanged in a crisis.

With cuffs of leopard-skin,
The fur of lamb he's in

---

① This song celebrated some officer of Zheng for his elegant appearance and integrity.

彼其之子，	那个人啊，
邦之司直。	掌管司法很正直。

羔裘晏①兮，	羊羔皮袍真鲜明，
三英②粲兮。	三道镶饰真美丽。
彼其之子，	那个人啊，
邦之彦③兮。	国中的才士文采异。

遵大路

遵大路兮，	沿着大路走啊，
掺④执子之祛兮。	拉着你的袖啊。
无我恶兮，	不要厌弃我啊，
不寁⑤故也。	不要这么快抛弃旧情啊。

遵大路兮，	沿着大路走啊，
掺执子之手兮。	拉着你的手啊。
无我魗⑥兮，	不要嫌我丑啊，
不寁好也。	不要这么快抛弃相好啊。

① 晏：鲜明的样子。
② 英：袍子上的饰纹。
③ 彦：士的美称。
④ 掺（shǎn）：执，拉着。
⑤ 寁（zǎn）：很快。
⑥ 魗（chǒu）：即"丑"。

Makes him look strong and bold;
To the right he will hold.

His fur of lamb is bright
With three stripes left and right.
The officer stands straight,
A hero of the State.

Leave Me Not[①]

I hold you by the sleeve
Along the public way.
O do not hate and leave
A mate of olden day!

I hold you by the hand
Along the public road.
Don't think me ugly and
Leave your former abode!

---

① A woman entreated her lover not to cast her off.

女曰鸡鸣

女曰鸡鸣，　　　　　　　　女人说："耳听鸡叫了。"
士曰昧旦[①]。　　　　　　　男人说："天才刚刚亮。"
子兴[②]视夜，　　　　　　　"你且起床看夜空，
明星[③]有烂。　　　　　　　启明星儿闪闪亮。
将翱将翔，　　　　　　　　请你快起来遨游啊，
弋凫与雁。　　　　　　　　射野鸭子也射雁。"

弋言加[④]之，　　　　　　　"射中鸭雁正正好，
与子宜[⑤]之。　　　　　　　给你烹了做美肴。
宜言饮酒，　　　　　　　　应该用来饮美酒，
与子偕老。　　　　　　　　与你一起相偕老。
琴瑟在御[⑥]，　　　　　　　你弹琴来我鼓瑟，
莫不静好。　　　　　　　　多么宁静又美好。"

知子之来[⑦]之，　　　　　　"知道你真关心我，
杂佩以赠之。　　　　　　　送你杂佩表我爱。
知子之顺之，　　　　　　　知道你真体贴我，
杂佩以问[⑧]之。　　　　　　送你杂佩表谢意。

---

① 昧旦：天色将亮未亮的时候。
② 兴：起来。
③ 明星：启明星。
④ 加：射中。
⑤ 宜：肴。
⑥ 御：协奏。
⑦ 来：关怀。
⑧ 问：慰问。

A Hunter's Domestic Life[①]

The wife says, "Cocks crow, hark!"
The man says, "It's still dark."
"Rise and see if it's night;
The morning star shines bright."
"Wild geese and ducks will fly;
I'll shoot them down from high."

"At shooting you are good;
I'll dress the game as food.
Together we'll drink wine
And live to ninety-nine.
With zither by our side,
In peace we shall abide."

"I know your wifely care;
I'll give you pearls to wear.
I know you will obey;
Can pearls and jade repay?

[①] A wife sent her husbnd from her side to his hunting and expressed her affection for him.

知子之好之,　　　　　　知道你真喜欢我,
杂佩以报之。　　　　　　送你杂佩表同心。"

有女同车

有女同车,　　　　　　　有个同车的姑娘,
颜如舜华①。　　　　　　脸儿美如木槿花。
将翱将翔,　　　　　　　我们一起遨游,
佩玉琼琚。　　　　　　　身戴佩环是美玉。
彼美孟姜,　　　　　　　美丽的孟家大姑娘,
洵美且都②！　　　　　　确实美丽又文雅!

有女同行,　　　　　　　有个同行的姑娘,
颜如舜英。　　　　　　　脸儿美如木槿花。
将翱将翔,　　　　　　　我们一起游玩,
佩玉将将。　　　　　　　身戴佩环响叮叮。
彼美孟姜,　　　　　　　美丽的孟家大姑娘,
德音不忘。　　　　　　　美好品德永明光。

山有扶苏

山有扶苏,　　　　　　　山上有桑树,
隰有荷华。　　　　　　　洼地有荷花。

---

① 舜华:同"舜英",木槿花。
② 都:闲雅。

I know your steadfast love;
I value nothing above."

Lady Jiang[①]

A lady in the cab with me
Looks like a flower from a hedge-tree.
She goes about as if in flight;
Her girdle-pendants look so bright.
O Lady Jiang with pretty face,
So elegant and full of grace!

The lady together with me
Walks like a blossoming hedge-tree.
She moves about as if in flight;
Her girdle-pendants tinkle light.
O Lady Jiang with pretty face,
Can I forget you so full of grace?

A Joke[②]

Uphill stands mulberry
And lotus in the pool.

[①] It was said that this was a praise of the newly-wed Lady Jiang.
[②] A woman mocked her lover as a sly fool.

不见子都，　　　　　　　　没有看见漂亮的子都，
乃见狂且①。　　　　　　　却看见一个轻狂小伙子。
山有桥松，　　　　　　　　山上有高松，
隰有游龙②。　　　　　　　洼地有荭草。
不见子充，　　　　　　　　没有看见漂亮的子充，
乃见狡童。　　　　　　　　却看见一个狡猾的小伙子。

萚③ 兮

萚兮萚兮，　　　　　　　　枯树枝啊枯树叶，
风其吹女。　　　　　　　　大风把你吹飘荡。
叔兮伯兮，　　　　　　　　老三啊老大啊，
倡④予和女。　　　　　　　你来领唱我来和。

萚兮萚兮，　　　　　　　　枯树枝啊枯树叶，
风其漂女。　　　　　　　　大风把你吹纷扬。
叔兮伯兮，　　　　　　　　老三啊老大啊，
倡予要女。　　　　　　　　你来起头我来和。

狡 童

彼狡童兮，　　　　　　　　那个小伙子太狡猾，
不与我言兮。　　　　　　　不再肯和我说话。

---

① 且：狂童。
② 游龙：荭草。
③ 萚（tuò）：枯树枝叶。
④ 倡：唱。

The handsome I don't see;
Instead I see a fool.
Uphill stands a pine-tree
And in the pool leaves red.
The pretty I don't see;
I see the sly instead.

Sing Together[①]

Leaves sear, leaves sear,
The wind blows you away.
Sing, cousins dear,
And I'll join in your lay.

Leaves sear, leaves sear,
The wind wafts you away.
Sing, cousins dear,
And I'll complete your lay.

A Handsome Guy[②]

You handsome guy
Won't speak to me words sweet.

---

① When leaves wafted in the wind after harvest, a songstress asked her companions to sing and dance together like wafting leaves.
② Some misunderstanding seemed to have arisen between the poetess and her handsome lover.

维[1]子之故,	因为你的缘故啊,
使我不能餐兮。	让我茶饭咽不下。

彼狡童兮,	那个小伙子太狡猾,
不与我食兮。	不再和我同吃饭。
维子之故,	因为你的缘故啊,
使我不能息兮。	让我睡觉都不安。

褰[2] 裳

子惠思我,	你若爱我想念我,
褰裳涉溱。	提起衣裳渡溱河。
子不我思,	你若变心不想我,
岂无他人?	难道无人爱我?
狂童之狂也且!	你这人儿太狂妄!

子惠思我,	你若爱我想念我,
褰裳涉洧。	提起衣裳过洧河。
子不我思,	你若变心不想我,
岂无他士?	难道无人爱我?
狂童之狂也且!	你这人儿太狂妄!

---

[1] 维:因为。
[2] 褰(qiān):提起。

For you I sigh
And can nor drink nor eat.

You handsome guy
Won't eat with me at my request.
For you I sigh
And cannot take my rest.

Lift up Your Robe[①]

If you think of me as you seem,
Lift up your robe and cross that stream!
If you don't love me as you seem,
Can I not find another one?
Your foolishness is second to none.

If you think of me as you seem,
Lift up your gown and cross this stream!
If you don't love me as you seem,
Can I not find another mate?
Your foolishness is really great.

---

① A woman sang to her lover who would not lift up his robe and cross the stream to meet her.

丰①

子之丰兮，	你的容貌丰润啊，
俟我乎巷兮。	等候我在里巷啊。
悔予不送兮。	后悔我没和你走啊！

子之昌②兮，	你的体魄多魁伟啊，
俟我乎堂兮。	等候我在堂屋啊。
悔予不将兮。	后悔我没同你行啊！

衣锦褧衣，	穿着锦衣罩单衣，
裳③锦褧裳。	穿着锦裙罩单裙。
叔兮伯兮，	大叔大伯啊，
驾予与行④！	驾车载我一起走！

裳锦褧裳，	穿着锦裙罩单裙，
衣锦褧衣。	穿着锦衣罩单衣。
叔兮伯兮，	大叔大伯啊，
驾予与归⑤！	驾车载我一同归！

① 丰：丰满。
② 昌：魁伟。
③ 裳：下裙。
④ 行：出嫁。
⑤ 归：出嫁。

Lost Opportunity[①]

You looked plump and plain
And waited for me in the lane.
Why did I not go with you? I complain.

You looked strong and tall
And waited for me in the hall.
I regret I did not return your call.

Over my broidered skirt
I put on simple shirt.
O Sir, to you I say:
Come in your cab and let us drive away!

I put on simple shirt
Over my broidered skirt.
O Sir, I say anew:
Come in your cab and take me home with you!

---

① A woman regretted that she had not kept her promise and wished that her lover would come again.

东门之墠①

东门之墠,　　　　　　　东门外面地平坦,
茹藘②在阪③。　　　　　茜草长在山坡上。
其室则迩,　　　　　　　她的房屋近咫尺,
其人甚远。　　　　　　　她的人儿远天涯。

东门之栗,　　　　　　　东门外面栗树下,
有践④家室。　　　　　　那有成排的村落。
岂不尔思?　　　　　　　难道我不想念你?
子不我即⑤。　　　　　　你却不与我亲近。

风 雨

风雨凄凄,　　　　　　　风凄凄雨泠泠,
鸡鸣喈喈。　　　　　　　喈喈鸡鸣不住声。
既见君子,　　　　　　　终于见到了君子,
云胡不夷⑥?　　　　　　怎么会不高兴。

风雨潇潇,　　　　　　　风凄凄雨潇潇,
鸡鸣胶胶。　　　　　　　胶胶鸡鸣不停叫。

---

① 墠(shàn):平坦的场地。
② 茹藘:茜草。
③ 阪:土坡。
④ 践:房屋排列整齐。
⑤ 即:靠近。
⑥ 夷:平,舒坦。

A Lover's Monologue①

At eastern gate on level ground
There are madder plants all around.
My lover's house is very near,
But far away he does appear.

'Neath chestnut tree at eastern gate
Within my house in vain I wait.
How can I not think of my dear?
Why won't he come to see me here?

Wind and Rain②

The wind and rain are chill;
The crow of cocks is shrill.
When I've seen my man best,
Should I not feel at rest?

The wind whistles with showers;
The cocks crow dreary hours.

---

① A woman thought of her lover and complained that he did not come to her though his house was very near, at the eastern gate of the capital of Zheng.
② This described the joy of a lonely wife on seeing her husband's return in wind and rain.

既见君子, 　　　　　　　　　终于见到了君子,
云胡不瘳①? 　　　　　　　　病怎么会还不好。

风雨如晦②, 　　　　　　　　风雨黑天暗地,
鸡鸣不已。 　　　　　　　　　鸡鸣还是不已。
既见君子, 　　　　　　　　　终于见到了君子,
云胡不喜? 　　　　　　　　　怎么会不欢喜。

子 衿③

青青子衿, 　　　　　　　　　青青的你的衣衫,
悠悠我心。 　　　　　　　　　长长挂在我的心间。
纵我不往, 　　　　　　　　　即使我不能去到你那里,
子宁不嗣④音? 　　　　　　　你怎么也不给我音讯?

青青子佩, 　　　　　　　　　青青的你的佩带,
悠悠我思。 　　　　　　　　　长长印在我的心间。
纵我不往, 　　　　　　　　　即使我不能去到你那里,
子宁不来? 　　　　　　　　　你怎么也不来到我这里?

挑兮达兮, 　　　　　　　　　我徘徊不安啊,
在城阙⑤兮。 　　　　　　　　在这城楼之上。

---

① 瘳(chōu):病愈。
② 晦:昏暗不明的样子。
③ 衿:衣领。
④ 嗣:寄。
⑤ 城阙:城楼上。

When I've seen my dear one,
With my ill could I not have done?

Gloomy wind and rain blend;
The cocks crow without end.
When I have seen my dear,
How full I feel of cheer!

To a Scholar[1]

Student with collar blue,
How much I long for you!
Though to see you I am not free,
O why don't you send word to me?

Scholar with belt-stone blue,
How long I think of you!
Though to see you I am not free,
O why don't you come to see me?

I'm pacing up and down
On the wall of the town.

---

[1] A woman longed for her lover.

一日不见,	一天看不见你,
如三月兮!	就像隔了三个月啊!

扬之水

扬之水,	舒缓的河水,
不流束楚。	一捆荆条漂不起。
终鲜兄弟,	既然没有兄弟,
维予与女。	只有我和你。
无信人之言,	不要听信别人的话,
人实迋①女。	人家是在哄骗你。

扬之水,	舒缓的河水,
不流束薪。	一捆柴草流不去。
终鲜兄弟,	既然没有兄弟,
维予二人。	只有我你二人。
无信人之言,	不要听信别人的话,
人实不信。	人家的话不能相信。

出其东门

出其东门,	走出东城门,
有女如云。	姑娘多如云。

---

① 迋（kuáng）：哄骗。

When to see you I am not free,
One day seems like three months to me.

Believe Me[1]

Wood bound together may
Not be carried away.
We have but brethren few;
There're only I and you.
What others say can't be believed,
Or you will be deceived.

A bundle of wood may
Not be carried away.
We have but brethren few;
There are only we two.
Do not believe what others say!
Untrustworthy are they.

My Lover in White[2]

Outside the eastern gate
Like clouds fair maidens date.

---

[1] A woman asserted good faith to her husband and protested against people who would make them doubt each other. A bundle of firewood might allude to a couple well united.
[2] A man praised his lover in white, contrasted with beautiful maidens dating outside the eastern gate of the capital of Zheng.

虽则如云，	虽然多如云，
匪我思存。	不是意中人。
缟①衣綦②巾，	白衣青巾人，
聊乐我员。	是我梦中人。
出其闉阇③，	走出外城郭，
有女如荼。	姑娘如花多。
虽则如荼，	虽然如花多，
匪我思且④。	不能打动我。
缟衣茹藘，	白衣红巾人，
聊可与娱。	是我梦中人。

野有蔓草

野有蔓草，	郊外野草蔓延，
零露漙⑤兮。	露水滴落浓浓。
有美一人，	有一位美人啊，
清扬婉兮。	眉清目秀好容颜。
邂逅⑥相遇，	不约而巧遇，
适我愿兮。	正合我的心愿。

---

① 缟：白色。
② 綦：青色。
③ 闉阇（yīn dū）：城外曲城的重门。
④ 且（cú）：往。
⑤ 漙（tuán）：露多。
⑥ 邂逅：不期而遇。

Though they are fair as cloud,
My love's not in the crowd.
Dressed in light green and white,
Alone she's my delight.

Outside the outer gate
Like blooms fair maidens date.
Though like blooms they are fair,
The one I love's not there.
Dressed in scarlet and white,
Alone she gives me delight.

The Creeping Grass[①]

Afield the creeping grass
With crystal dew o'erspread,
There's a beautiful lass
With clear eyes and fine forehead.
When I meet the clear-eyed,
My desire's satisfied.

---

① This song described the love-making of a young man and a beautiful lass amid the creeping grass o'erspread with morning dew.

野有蔓草，	郊外野草蔓延，
零露瀼瀼①。	露水滴落晶莹。
有美一人，	有一位美人啊，
婉如清扬。	眉清目秀有风情。
邂逅相遇，	不约而巧遇，
与子偕臧。	我们都很快乐。

溱 洧

溱与洧，	溱水和洧水，
方涣涣兮。	正在哗哗淌。
士与女，	小伙儿和姑娘，
方秉蕑②兮。	手握兰草香。
女曰："观乎？"	姑娘说："去看看吧？"
士曰："既且。"	小伙子说："已经看过了。"
"且往观乎。	"再去看看也好。"
洧之外，	洧水的边上，
洵訏③且乐。"	地方宽敞人快乐。"
维士与女，	男女相伴，
伊其相谑，	你说说我笑笑，
赠之以勺药。	送你一把芍药。

① 瀼瀼（ráng ráng）：露多。
② 蕑（jiān）：兰草。
③ 訏（xū）：大。

Afield the creeping grass
With round dewdrops o'erspread,
There's a beautiful lass
With clear eyes and fine forehead.
When I meet the clear-eyed,
Amid the grass let's hide!

Riverside Rendezvous[①]

The Rivers Zhen and Wei
Overflow on their way.
The lovely lad and lass
Hold in hand fragrant grass.
"Let's look around," says she;
"I've already," says he.

"Let us go there again!
Beyond the River Wei
The ground is large and people gay."
Playing together then,
They have a happy hour;
Each gives the other peony flower.

---

① It was the custom of the State of Zheng for young people to meet and make love by the riverside on the festive day of the third lunar month in spring.

溱与洧,	溱水和洧水,
浏其清矣。	清澈能见底。
士与女,	小伙儿和姑娘,
殷①其盈矣。	拥拥攘攘多热闹。
女曰:"观乎?"	姑娘说:"去看看吧?"
士曰:"既且。"	小伙子说:"已经看过了。"
"且往观乎,	"再去看一下也好,
洧之外,	洧水的边上,
洵訏且乐。"	地方宽敞人喜悦。"
维士与女,	男女相伴,
伊其相谑,	你说说我笑笑,
赠之以勺药。	送你一把芍药。

① 殷:众多。

The Rivers Zhen and Wei
Flow crystal-clear;
Lad and lass squeeze their way
Through the crowd full of cheer.
"Let's look around," says she;
"I've already," says he.

"Let us go there again!
Beyond the River Wei
The ground is large and people gay."
Playing together then,
They have a happy hour;
Each gives the other peony flower.

齐 风

鸡 鸣

"鸡既鸣矣,
朝① 既盈矣。"
"匪鸡则鸣,
苍蝇之声。"

"东方明矣,
朝既昌② 矣。"
"匪东方则明,
月出之光。"

"虫飞薨薨③,
甘与子同梦。"
"会④ 且归矣,
无庶予子憎。"

"听见鸡叫了,
朝堂上的人该满了。"
"不是鸡在叫,
那是苍蝇闹。"

"看见东方亮了,
朝堂上的人该从了。"
"不是东方亮了,
是月亮发出的光。"

"虫飞嗡嗡嗡,
我愿和你同入梦。"
"朝会都要散啦,
别因我而被人憎。"

① 朝:朝堂。
② 昌:盛多。
③ 薨薨:虫子成群飞鸣声。
④ 会:朝会。

Songs Collected in Qi, Modern Shandong

A Courtier and His Wife[①]

"Wake up!" she says, "Cocks crow.
The court is on the go."
"It's not the cock that cries,"
He says, "but humming flies."

"The east is brightening;
The court is in full swing."
"It's not the east that's bright
But the moon shedding light."

"See buzzing insects fly.
It's sweet in bed to lie.
But courtiers will not wait;
None likes you to be late."

---

① This was a dialogue between a courtier and his wife. It was said that the dialogue might refer to the marquess of Qi (934—894 B. C.) and the marchioness.

还

子之还①兮，	你真轻捷啊，
遭我乎峱②之间兮。	遇逢我在峱山间。
并驱从③两肩④兮，	并排驱赶两只兽，
揖我谓我儇⑤兮。	你作揖夸我好身手。
子之茂⑥兮，	你真壮健啊，
遭我乎峱之道兮。	遇逢我在峱山道上。
并驱从两牡兮，	并排驱赶两公兽，
揖我谓我好兮。	你作揖夸我好样的。
子之昌兮，	你真强壮啊，
遭我乎峱之阳兮。	遇逢我在峱山南边。
并驱从两狼兮，	并排驱赶两只狼，
揖我谓我臧兮。	作揖夸我好善良。

① 还（xuán）：轻捷的样子。
② 峱（náo）：齐国山名，在今山东省。
③ 从：追逐。
④ 肩：三岁的兽。
⑤ 儇（xuān）：灵利。
⑥ 茂：健美，强壮。

Two Hunters[①]

How agile you appear!
Amid the hills we meet.
Pursuing two boars, compeer,
You bow and say I'm fleet.

How skilful you appear!
We meet halfway uphill.
Driving after two males, compeer,
You bow and praise my skill.

How artful you appear!
South of the hill we meet.
Pursuing two wolves, compeer,
You bow and say my art's complete.

① This was the compliments interchanged by two hunters of Qi. Some critics said that this was a specimen of admirable satire, through which the boastful manners of the people of Qi were clearly exhibited.

著①

俟②我于著乎而，	等我就在门屏间，
充耳以素乎而，	冠垂白挂丝耳边，
尚之以琼华③乎而。	添加上红玉更明显！
俟我于庭乎而，	等我就在院子间，
充耳以青乎而，	冠垂青丝在耳边，
尚之以琼莹乎而。	添加上红玉更美艳！
俟我于堂乎而，	等我就在堂屋间，
充耳以黄乎而，	冠垂黄丝在耳边，
尚之以琼英乎而。	添加上红玉更光鲜！

东方之日

东方之日兮，	东方的太阳啊，
彼姝④者子，	那个美丽的姑娘，
在我室兮。	在我的房间啊。
在我室兮，	在我的房间啊，
履我即兮。	伴我意浓情长。

---

① 著：门屏间。
② 俟：等待。
③ 琼华：美玉，下"琼莹""琼英"同。
④ 姝：美女。

The Bridegroom[1]

He waits for me between the door and screen,
His crown adorned with ribbons green
Ended with gems of beautiful sheen.

He waits for me in the court with delight,
His crown adorned with ribbons white
Ended with gems and rubies bright.

He waits for me in inner hall,
His crown adorned with yellow ribbons all
Ended with gems like golden ball.

Nocturnal Tryst[2]

The eastern sun is red;
The maiden like a bloom
Follows me to my room.
The maiden in my room
Follows me to the bed.

---

[1] A bride described her first meeting with the bridegroom who should wait for her arrival first at the door, then in the court and at last in the inner hall, according to ancient nuptial ceremony.

[2] The maiden came to the tryst like the eastern sun and left her lover like the eastern moon.

东方之月兮，　　　东方的月亮啊，
彼姝者子，　　　　那个美丽的姑娘，
在我闼①兮。　　　在我的门旁啊。
在我闼兮，　　　　在我的门旁啊，
履我发兮。　　　　随我情浓意长。

东方未明

东方未明，　　　　东方没有亮，
颠倒衣裳。　　　　颠颠倒倒穿衣裳。
颠之倒之，　　　　穿反了，穿倒了，
自公召之。　　　　公爷紧急要召见。

东方未晞②，　　　东方没有光，
颠倒裳衣。　　　　颠颠倒倒穿衣裳。
倒之颠之，　　　　穿反了，穿倒了，
自公令之。　　　　公爷命令心急慌。

折柳樊圃，　　　　攀折柳条编园篱，
狂夫③瞿瞿④。　　狂妄监工眼盯着。
不能辰夜，　　　　白昼黑夜难分清，
不夙则莫。　　　　不是凌晨即暮昏。

① 闼：门。
② 晞：破晓的时候。
③ 狂夫：指狂妄的监工。
④ 瞿瞿（jù jù）：惊惧怒视的样子。

The eastern moon is bright;
The maiden I adore
Follows me out of door.
The maiden out of door
Leaves me and goes out of sight.

A Tryst before Dawn[①]

Before the east sees dawn,
You put on clothes upside down.
O upside down you put them on,
For orders come from ducal crown.

Before the east is bright,
You take the left sleeve for the right.
You put in left sleeve your right arm,
For orders bring disorder and alarm.

Don't leave my garden fence with willow tree;
Do not stare at my naked body, please.
You either come too late at night,
Or leave me early in twilight.

[①] A toiler complained of the early rise before dawn and the disorder brought by the order of the duke and the supervisor.

南 山

南山崔崔,　　　　　　　　巍巍南山势高峻,
雄狐绥绥①。　　　　　　　雄狐慢慢寻雌狐。
鲁道有荡②,　　　　　　　 鲁国大道势平坦,
齐子由归。　　　　　　　　齐国女子从此嫁。
既曰归止,　　　　　　　　既然已经嫁出去,
曷又怀止?　　　　　　　　为什么还要想着她?

葛屦五两③,　　　　　　　 葛鞋排列排成双,
冠緌④双止。　　　　　　　帽带一对双垂下。
鲁道有荡,　　　　　　　　鲁国大道势平坦,
齐子庸止。　　　　　　　　齐国女子从此嫁。
既曰庸止,　　　　　　　　既然已经嫁出去,
曷又从止?　　　　　　　　为什么还要盯着她?

① 绥绥：求偶相随的样子。
② 荡：平坦。
③ 五两：排列成双。
④ 緌（ruí）：帽带。

Incest[1]

To Duke Xiang of Qi

The southern hill is great;
A male fox seeks his mate.
The way to Lu is plain;
Your sister with her train
Goes to wed Duke of Lu.
Why should you go there too?

The shoes are made in pairs
And strings of gems she wears.
The way to Lu is plain;
Your sister goes to reign
And wed with Duke of Lu.
Why should you follow her too?

---

[1] This was a satire against Duke Xiang of Qi and Duke Huan of Lu. In 708 B. C. Duke Huan married a daughter of Qi, known as Wen Jiang. There was an improper affection between her and her brother, Duke Xiang; and on his succession to Qi, the couple visited him. The consequences were incest between the brother and sister, the murder of the husband and a disgraceful connection, long continued, between the guilty pair. In the first stanza, the great southern hill alluded to the great State of Qi and the male fox seeking his mate alluded contemptuously to Duke Xiang seeking his sister who was going to wed Duke Huan of Lu. In the second stanza, the shoes and strings of gems made in pairs alluded to the union of man and wife. In the third stanza, the ground well prepared for hemp alluded to the preparations for marriage between Duke Huan and Wen Jiang. In the last stanza, the splitting of firewood was a formality in contracting a marriage during the Zhou dynasty.

蓺麻如之何？	怎么想要种大麻？
衡从其亩。	田亩横纵有其法。
取妻如之何？	青年怎么娶妻子？
必告父母。	必先告诉父母家。
既曰告止，	已经告诉父母家，
曷又鞠①止？	为什么还要放纵她？
析薪如之何？	怎么劈柴砍木头？
匪斧不克。	不用斧头不能做。
取妻如之何？	迎娶妻子靠什么？
匪媒不得。	没有媒人得不到。
既曰得止，	已经娶到妻子了，
曷又极②止？	为什么还要放任她？

甫③ 田

无田甫田，	不要耕种主家大田，
维莠④骄骄。	只有狗尾草长得高。
无思远人，	不要想念远方的人，
劳心忉忉⑤。	想念使人更心伤。

① 鞠（jū）：放纵。
② 极：放任到了极点。
③ 甫：大。
④ 莠：狗尾草。
⑤ 忉忉（dāo dāo）：忧伤的样子。

To Duke Huan of Lu

For hemp the ground is ploughed and dressed
From north to south, from east to west.
When a wife comes to your household,
Your parents should be told.
If you told your father and mother,
Should your wife go back to her brother?

How is the firewood split?
An axe can sever it.
How can a wife be won?
With go-between it's done.
To be your wife she's vowed;
No incest is allowed.

Missing Her Son[①]

Don't till too large a ground,
Or weed will spread around.
Don't miss one far away,
Or you'll grieve night and day.

---

① It was said that the song was written for Wen Jiang of Qi (See the preceding poem) missing her son who became Duke Zhuang of Lu at the age of thirteen.

无田甫田,	不要耕种主家大田,
维莠桀桀。	只有狗尾草长得旺。
无思远人,	不要想念远方的人,
劳心怛怛①。	想念使人更悲伤。
婉兮娈兮,	清秀啊漂亮啊,
总角丱②兮。	两束小辫像羊角。
未几见兮,	几时没有见到他,
突而弁③兮。	突然戴上成人帽。

卢④ 令

卢令令,	猎狗颈铃响当当,
其人美且仁。	那人漂亮好心肠。
卢重环,	猎狗颈铃带双环,
其人美且鬈⑤。	那人漂亮头发卷。

---

① 怛怛（dá dá）：悲伤的样子。
② 丱（guàn）：小孩子梳两个辫子，也叫总角。
③ 弁：帽子。
④ 卢：猎狗。
⑤ 鬈：头发卷曲。

Don't till too large a ground,
Or weed overgrows around.
Don't miss the far-off one,
Or your grief won't be done.

My son was young and fair
With his two tufts of hair.
Not seen for a short time,
He's grown up to his prime.

Hunter and Hounds[1]

The bells of hound
Give ringing sound;
Its master's mind
Is good and kind.

The good hound brings
Its double rings;
Its master's hair
Is curled and fair.

---

[1] This was a description of a handsome hunter. It was said that this was a satire against Duke Xiang's wild addiction to handsome to the detriment of public interest.

卢重鋂[1], 　　　　　　　　　猎狗颈铃是双铃，
其人美且偲[2]。 　　　　　　　那人漂亮又多才。

敝　笱[3]

敝笱在梁， 　　　　　　　　　破鱼篓在鱼梁上，
其鱼鲂鳏。 　　　　　　　　　鳊鱼鲲鱼在游荡。
齐子归止， 　　　　　　　　　齐国的女子回国去，
其从如云。 　　　　　　　　　前呼后拥云一样。

敝笱在梁， 　　　　　　　　　破鱼篓在鱼梁上，
其鱼鲂鱮。 　　　　　　　　　鳊鱼鲢鱼意洋洋。
齐子归止， 　　　　　　　　　齐国的女子回国去，
其从如雨。 　　　　　　　　　前呼后拥雨一样。

敝笱在梁， 　　　　　　　　　破鱼篓在鱼梁上，
其鱼唯唯[4]。 　　　　　　　　鱼儿游来又游往。
齐子归止， 　　　　　　　　　齐国的女子回国去，
其从如水。 　　　　　　　　　前呼后拥像水一样。

① 鋂（méi）：一大环套两个小环。
② 偲（cāi）：多才。
③ 笱（gǒu）：鱼篓。
④ 唯唯：鱼儿相随游行的样子。

The good hound brings
Its triple rings;
Its master's beard
Is deep revered.

Duchess Wen Jiang of Qi[1]

The basket is worn out
And fishes swim about.
The duchess comes with crowd,
Capricious like the cloud.

The basket is worn out;
Bream and tench swim about.
The duchess comes like flower,
Inconstant like the shower.

The basket is worn out;
Fish swim freely about.
Here comes Duke of Qi's daughter,
Changeable like water.

---

[1] The worn-out basket unable to catch fish alluded to Duke Huan of Lu unable to control the bold licentious conduct of his wife Wen Jiang in returning to the State of Qi(See the Note on Poem "Incest").

载 驱

载驱薄薄①,　　　　　　　　车马快走拍拍响,
簟②茀③朱鞹④。　　　　　　竹席车帘红皮帐。
鲁道有荡,　　　　　　　　鲁国大路真平坦,
齐子发夕。　　　　　　　　齐女夜归把车上。

四骊⑤济济,　　　　　　　　四匹黑马多强壮,
垂辔沵沵⑥。　　　　　　　缰绳垂下多舒畅。
鲁道有荡,　　　　　　　　鲁国大路真平坦,
齐子岂弟⑦。　　　　　　　齐女乘车天将亮。

汶水汤汤,　　　　　　　　汶水涨得汪洋洋,
行人彭彭。　　　　　　　　路上行人熙攘攘。
鲁道有荡,　　　　　　　　鲁国大路真平坦,
齐子翱翔。　　　　　　　　齐女在此闲游逛。

汶水滔滔,　　　　　　　　汶水流得浩荡荡,
行人儦儦⑧。　　　　　　　路上行人跄跄跄。
鲁道有荡,　　　　　　　　鲁国大路真平坦,
齐子游敖。　　　　　　　　齐女在此自遨荡。

① 薄薄：车马走得很快的声音。
② 簟（diàn）：竹席。
③ 茀（fú）：车帘。
④ 朱鞹（kuò）：红色的去毛的兽皮。
⑤ 骊：黑色的马。
⑥ 沵沵（nǐ nǐ）：柔和舒畅，指驾技高。
⑦ 岂（kǎi）弟：天刚亮。
⑧ 儦儦（biāo biāo）：人多的样子。

Duke of Qi and Duchess of Lu[①]

The duke's cab drives ahead
With screens of leather red;
The duchess starts her way
Before the break of day.

The duke's steeds run amain;
Soft looks their hanging rein.
The duchess speeds her way
At the break of the day.

The river flows along;
Travellers come in throng.
Duke and duchess meet by day
And make merry all the way.

The river's overflowed
With travellers in crowd.
Duke and duchess all day
Make merry all the way.

---

① This was a satire against the open shamelessness of Duchess of Wen Jiang of Lu in her meeting with her brother, Duke Xiang of Qi. The merry-making might allude to their love-making (See Note on Poem "Incest").

猗 嗟[1]

猗嗟昌兮!	啊呀,真精壮啊!
颀而长兮!	身材高而长啊!
抑若扬兮!	额头丰满真漂亮啊!
美目扬兮!	眼睛上扬真明亮啊!
巧趋跄[2]兮!	步伐多矫健啊!
射则臧兮!	射箭多熟练啊!
猗嗟名兮!	啊呀,真漂亮啊!
美目清兮!	眼目真清澈啊!
仪既成兮!	仪容已成就啊!
终日射侯[3],	整日射箭靶啊!
不出正[4]兮!	不出正中心啊!
展[5]我甥兮!	真是个好外甥啊!
猗嗟娈兮!	啊呀,真美好啊!
清扬婉兮!	眼睛清澈明媚啊!
舞则选[6]兮!	舞姿多出色啊!
射则贯[7]兮!	射箭中靶心啊!
四矢反[8]兮!	四箭中一点啊!
以御乱兮!	用来抵御叛乱啊!

[1] 猗(yī)嗟:赞叹的语气词。
[2] 趋跄:行走矫健有节奏。
[3] 侯:箭靶。
[4] 正:箭靶正中心。
[5] 展:真正的。
[6] 选:合节拍。
[7] 贯:射中而穿透。
[8] 反:复,一次次。

The Archer Duke[①]

Fairest of all,
He's grand and tall,
His forehead high
With sparkling eye;
He's fleet of foot
And skilled to shoot.

His fame is high
With crystal eye;
In brave array
He shoots all day;
Each shot a hit,
No son's so fit.

He's fair and bright
With keenest sight;
He dances well;
Each shot will tell;
Four shots right go;
He'll quell the foe.

① This song referred to Duke Zhuang of Lu, son of Duchess Wen Jiang and nephew of Duke Xiang of Qi.

魏 风

葛 屦

纠纠①葛屦，	缠缠绕绕编草鞋，
可②以履霜？	如何用它踩秋霜？
掺掺③女手，	纤纤细细姑娘手，
可以缝裳？	如何能够缝衣裳？
要④之襋⑤之，	缝好衣纽缝衣领，
好人服之。	贵人试穿新衣裳。

好人提提⑥，	贵人走路好傲慢，
宛然左辟，	都闪左边把路让，
佩其象揥⑦。	象牙簪子头上戴。
维是褊心，	真是偏心不公平，
是以为刺。	因此讽刺把歌唱。

① 纠纠：缠绕。
② 可（hé）：何，怎么。
③ 掺掺（xiān xiān）：纤细瘦弱。
④ 要（yāo）：衣纽。
⑤ 襋（jí）：衣领。
⑥ 提提：傲慢的样子。
⑦ 揥（tì）：簪子。

Songs Collected in Wei, Modern Shanxi

A Well-Drest Lady and Her Maid[1]

In summer shoes with silken lace,
A maid walks on frost at quick pace.
By slender fingers of the maid
Her mistress' beautiful attire is made.
The waistband and the collar fair
Are ready now for her mistress to wear.

The lady moves with pride;
She turns her head aside
With ivory pins in her hair.
Against her narrow mind
I'll use satire unkind.

---

[1] This was a satire against a well-dressed lady and a praise of her sewing maid.

汾沮洳[1]

彼汾沮洳，	汾水岸边湿地上，
言采其莫[2]。	采那里的酸模忙。
彼其之子，	那个采摘酸模的人，
美无度。	美得难衡量。
美无度，	美得难衡量，
殊异乎公路[3]。	管公家车的将军比不上。
彼汾一方，	汾水河岸斜坡旁，
言采其桑。	采那里的饲蚕桑。
彼其之子，	那个采摘蚕桑的人，
美如英。	美得如花放。
美如英，	美得如花放，
殊异乎公行[4]。	管公家战车的将军比不上。
彼汾一曲，	汾水曲曲水湾浜，
言采其藚[5]。	采那里的泽泻香。
彼其之子，	那个采摘泽泻的人，
美如玉。	美得如玉样。
美如玉，	美得如玉样，
殊异乎公族[6]。	管公家属车的将军比不上。

① 沮洳（jù rù）：低湿地。
② 莫：酸模，可以食用。
③ 公路：管公家车子的将军。
④ 公行：管公家战车的将军。
⑤ 藚（xù）：泽泻，可以入药。
⑥ 公族：管公家属车的将军。

A Scholar Unknown[1]

By riverside, alas!
A scholar gathers grass.
He gathers grass at leisure,
Careful beyond measure,
Beyond measure his grace,
Why not in a high place?

By riverside picks he
The leaves of mulberry.
Amid the leaves he towers
As brilliant as flowers.
Such brilliancy and beauty,
Why not on official duty?

By riverside he trips
To gather the ox-tips.
His virtue not displayed
Like deeply buried jade.
His virtue once appears,
He would surpass his peers.

[1] This was a criticism of the State of Wei where only wealthy lords could be high officials while brilliant scholars could only gather grass and leaves without any official duty.

园有桃

园有桃,　　　　　　　　园中有桃树,
其实之殽①。　　　　　　桃子可以吃。
心之忧矣,　　　　　　　心里很忧伤,
我歌且谣。　　　　　　　只能唱歌谣。
不知我者,　　　　　　　不了解我的人,
谓我士也骄。　　　　　　说士人太骄傲。
彼人是哉,　　　　　　　那个人说的对吗,
子曰何其?"　　　　　　你说又能怎么样?
心之忧矣,　　　　　　　心里忧伤啊,
其谁知之?　　　　　　　谁能了解我?
其谁知之,　　　　　　　谁能了解我,
盖亦勿思!　　　　　　　还是不要去想它!

园有棘,　　　　　　　　园中有枣树,
其实之食。　　　　　　　枣子可以吃。
心之忧矣,　　　　　　　心里很忧伤,
聊以行国。　　　　　　　只能去游荡。
不知我者,　　　　　　　不了解我的人,
谓我士也罔极②。　　　　说士人太偏激。
彼人是哉,　　　　　　　那个人说的对吗,
子曰何其?　　　　　　　你说又能怎么样?

① 殽:即"肴",指可以吃。
② 罔极:无正中之道。

A Scholar Misunderstood[1]

Fruit of peach tree
Is used as food.
It saddens me
To sing and brood.
Who knows me not
Says I am proud.
He's right in what?
Tell me aloud.
I'm full of woes
My heart would sink,
But no one knows,
For none will think,

Of garden tree
I eat the date.
It saddens me
To roam the state.
Who knows me not
Says I am queer.
He's right in what?
O let me hear!

---

[1] This was another criticism of the State of Wei where unemployed poor scholars used peach and date as food.

心之忧矣,	心里忧伤啊,
其谁知子?	谁能了解我?
其谁知之,	谁能了解我,
盖亦勿思!	还是不要去想它!

陟 岵[①]

陟彼岵兮,	登上那座青山啊,
瞻望父兮。	眺望家中父亲啊。
父曰:"嗟!	父亲好像正在说:"唉,
予子行役,	我的儿子在服役。
夙夜无已。	日日夜夜不停歇。
上慎旃[②]哉,	还是千万小心啊,
犹来无止!"	可以回来不停留!"

陟彼屺[③]兮,	登上那座秃山啊,
瞻望母兮。	眺望家中母亲啊。
母曰:"嗟!	母亲好像正在说:"唉!
予季行役,	我的小儿子在服役,
夙夜无寐。	日日夜夜无安眠。
上慎旃哉,	还是千万小心啊,
犹来无弃!"	可以回来不放弃。"

① 岵(hù):有草木的山。
② 旃:之,助词。
③ 屺(qǐ):没有草木的山。

I'm full of woes;
My heart would sink.
But no one knows,
For none will think.

A Homesick Soldier[1]

I climb the hill covered with grass
And look towards where my parents stay.
My father would say, "Alas!
My son's on service far away;
He cannot rest night and day.
O may he take good care
To come back and not remain there!"

I climb the hill devoid of grass
And look towards where my parents stay.
My mother would say, "Alas!
My youngest son's on service far away;
He cannot sleep well night and day.
O may he take good care
To come back and not be captive there!"

---

[1] A young soldier on service solaced himself with the thought of home.

陟彼冈兮，	登上那座山岗啊，
瞻望兄兮。	眺望家中兄长啊。
兄曰："嗟！	兄长好像正在说："唉！
予弟行役，	我的弟弟在服役，
夙夜必偕①。	与人军营里。
上慎旃哉，	还是要小心啊，
犹来无死！"	可以回来不世弃！"

十亩之间

十亩之间兮，	一块桑园十亩大啊，
桑者闲闲兮。	采桑人儿真悠闲啊。
行与子还兮。	我要与你同回去啊。

十亩之外兮，	一块桑园十多亩，
桑者泄泄②兮。	采桑人儿真自在啊。
行与子逝兮。	我要与你同回去啊。

伐 檀

坎坎③伐檀兮，	砍伐檀树满山响啊，
寘④之河之干⑤兮，	把它放在河岸上啊。

---

① 偕：与行伍的兄弟们一起。
② 泄泄（yì yì）：轻松自在的样子。
③ 坎坎：砍伐木头的声音。
④ 寘：即"置"，安放。
⑤ 干：河岸。

I climb the hilltop green with grass
And look towards where my brothers stay.
My eldest brother would say, "Alas!
My youngest brother is on service far away;
He stays with comrades night and day.
O may he take good care
To come back and not be killed there!"

Gathering Mulberry[①]

Among ten acres of mulberry
All the planters are free.
Why not come back with me?

Beyond ten acres of mulberry
All the lasses are free.
O come away with me!

The Woodcutter's Song[②]

Chop, chop our blows on elm-trees go;
On rivershore we pile the wood.

[①] This was a song sung by a planter of mulberry trees to a lass after the gathering of mulberries.
[②] This was a satire against those idle and greedy lords of the state.

河水清且涟①猗。　　　　　　　河水清澈起波澜啊，
不稼②不穑③，　　　　　　　　不耕种啊不收获，
胡取禾三百廛④兮？　　　　　　凭什么有禾三百束啊？
不狩⑤不猎，　　　　　　　　　不上山啊去打猎，
胡瞻尔庭有县貆兮？　　　　　　为什么你的庭内挂貆肉啊？
彼君子兮，　　　　　　　　　　那些君子大人啊，
不素餐⑥兮！　　　　　　　　　全都是在吃白饭啊！

坎坎伐辐兮，　　　　　　　　　砍伐檀树制车辐啊，
寘之河之侧兮，　　　　　　　　把它放在河边上啊，
河水清且直猗。　　　　　　　　河水清澈又顺直啊。
不稼不穑，　　　　　　　　　　不耕种啊不收获，
胡取禾三百亿⑦兮？　　　　　　凭什么有禾三百束啊？
不狩不猎，　　　　　　　　　　不上山啊去打猎，
胡瞻尔庭有县特⑧兮？　　　　　为什么你的庭内挂兽肉啊？
彼君子兮，　　　　　　　　　　那些君子大人啊，
不素食兮！　　　　　　　　　　全都是在白吃饭啊！

坎坎伐轮兮，　　　　　　　　　砍下檀树做车轮啊，
寘之河之漘⑨兮，　　　　　　　把它放在河边上啊，

---

① 涟：风吹形成的水纹。
② 稼：种庄稼。
③ 穑（sè）：收庄稼。
④ 廛：束。
⑤ 狩：冬天打猎。
⑥ 素餐：白吃饭，不劳而食。
⑦ 亿：束。
⑧ 特：野兽。
⑨ 漘（chún）：河岸。

The clear and rippling waters flow.
How can those who nor reap nor sow
Have three hundred sheaves of corn in their place?
How can those who nor hunt nor chase
Have in their courtyard badgers of each race?
Those lords are good
Who do not need work for food!

Chop, chop, our blows for wheel-spokes go;
By riverside we pile the wood.
The clear and even waters flow.
How can those who nor reap nor sow
Have three millions of sheaves in their place?
How can those who nor hunt nor chase
Have in their courtyard games of each race?
Those lords are good
Who need no work to eat theirfood!

Chop, chop our blows for the wheels go;
At river brink we pile the wood.

河水清且沦①猗。	河水清澈起微澜啊。
不稼不穑，	不耕种啊不收获，
胡取禾三百囷②兮？	凭什么有禾三百束啊？
不狩不猎，	不上山啊去打猎，
胡瞻尔庭有县鹑兮？	为什么你的庭内挂着鹌鹑肉啊？
彼君子兮，	那些君子大人啊，
不素飧③兮！	全都是在白吃饭啊！

硕④ 鼠

硕鼠硕鼠，	大老鼠啊大老鼠，
无食我黍！	不要吃我种的黍！
三岁贯⑤女，	三年辛苦养活你，
莫我肯顾。	你却没有顾及我。
逝⑥将去⑦女，	发誓从此离开你，
适⑧彼乐土。	到那理想乐土去。
乐土乐土，	乐土啊乐土，
爰得我所！	才是我的好归处！
硕鼠硕鼠，	大老鼠啊大老鼠，
无食我麦！	不要吃我种的麦。

① 沦：水上的微波。
② 囷（qūn）：捆。
③ 飧（sūn）：晚餐。
④ 硕：大。
⑤ 贯：养活。
⑥ 逝：发誓。
⑦ 去：离开。
⑧ 适：往，到。

The clear and dimpling waters flow.
How can those who nor reap nor sow
Have three hundred ricks of corn in their place?
How can those who nor hunt nor chase
Have in their courtyard winged games of each race?
Those lords are good
Who do not have to work for food!

Large Rat[①]

Large rat, large rat,
Eat no more millet we grow!
Three years you have grown fat;
No care for us you show.
We'll leave you now, I swear,
For a happier land,
A happier land where
We may have a free hand.

Large rat, large rat,
Eat no more wheat we grow!

[①] The large rat was symbolic of the corrupt official and the happier land or state was a Utopia of the peasants.

三岁贯女,	三年辛苦养活你,
莫我肯德。	你却没有些感激。
逝将去女,	发誓从此离开你,
适彼乐国。	到那理想乐国去。
乐国乐国,	乐国啊乐国,
爰得我直①!	才能劳而有所获! |// blank
硕鼠硕鼠,	大老鼠啊大老鼠,
无食我苗!	不要吃我种的苗。
三岁贯女,	三年辛苦养活你,
莫我肯劳②。	却没有些慰劳。
逝将去女,	发誓从此离开你,
适彼乐郊。	到那理想乐郊去。
乐郊乐郊,	乐郊啊乐郊,
谁之永号!	抒发郁闷长呼号!

① 直:价值。
② 劳:慰劳。

Three years you have grown fat;
No kindness to us you show.
We'll leave you now, I swear,
For a happier state,
A happier state where
We can decide our fate.

Large rat, large rat,
Eat no more rice we grow!
Three years you have grown fat;
No rewards to our labor go.
We'll leave you now, I swear,
For a happier plain,
A happier plain where
None will groan or complain.

唐 风

蟋 蟀

蟋蟀在堂,
岁聿其莫①。
今我不乐,
日月其除②。
无已大康③,
职④思其居⑤。
好乐无荒,
良士瞿瞿⑥。

蟋蟀已经入堂屋,
一年就要过完了。
今天我不及时乐,
时光将去不复返。
不要过分地行乐,
常思地位和责任。
寻乐不能荒正业,
良士警惕事变化。

蟋蟀在堂,
岁聿其逝⑦。
今我不乐,
日月其迈⑧。
无已大康,
职思其外。

蟋蟀已经入堂屋,
一年就要结束了。
今天我不及时乐,
时光将逝不复还。
不要过分地行乐,
常思地位和责任。

① 莫:即"暮",晚。
② 除:流逝,过去。
③ 大康:安乐康泰。
④ 职:常。
⑤ 居:所处的地位,所处之事。
⑥ 瞿瞿:警惕四顾的样子。
⑦ 逝:过去。
⑧ 迈:消逝。

Songs Collected in Tang, Modern Shanxi

The Cricket[1]

The cricket chirping in the hall,
The year will pass away.
The present not enjoyed at all,
We'll miss the passing day.
Do not enjoy to excess
But do our duty with delight!
We'll enjoy ourselves none the less
If we see those at left and right.

The cricket chirping in the hall,
The year will go away.
The present not enjoyed at all,
We'll miss the bygone day.
Do not enjoy to excess
But only to the full extent!

---

[1] We might see in this song the cheerfulness and discretion of the people of Jin and their tempered enjoyment at fitting seasons.

好乐无荒,	寻乐不能荒正业,
良士蹶蹶①。	良士努力勤做事。

蟋蟀在堂,	蟋蟀已经入堂屋,
役车其休。	服役的车儿停下了。
今我不乐,	今天我不及时乐,
日月其慆②。	时光将永不再来。
无已大康。	不要过分地行乐,
职思其忧。	常思谋事多有忧。
好乐无荒,	寻乐不能荒正业,
良士休休③。	良士安然心坦荡。

山有枢

山有枢,	山上有枢树,
隰有榆。	洼地有榆树。
子有衣裳,	你有上衣和下裙,
弗曳④弗娄⑤。	不穿也不着。
子有车马,	你有车辆和马匹,
弗驰弗驱。	不驾也不赶。
宛⑥其死矣,	要是一天死去了,
他人是愉。	别人一定很高兴。

① 蹶蹶(guì guì):敏捷奋进的样子。
② 慆(tāo):逝去。
③ 休休:安然自得的样子。
④ 曳(yè):拖。
⑤ 娄:提。
⑥ 宛:枯萎。

We'll enjoy ourselves none the less
If we are diligent.

The cricket chirping by the door,
Our cart stands unemployed.
The year will be no more
With the days unenjoyed.
Do not enjoy to excess
But think of hidden sorrow!
We'll enjoy ourselves none the less
If we think of tomorrow.

Why Not Enjoy? [1]

Uphill you have elm-trees;
Downhill you have elms white.
You have dress as you please.
Why not wear it with delight?
You have horses and car.
Why don't you take a ride?
One day when dead you are,
Others will drive them with pride.

---

[1] This was a satire on the folly of not enjoying the good things and letting death put them into the hands of others.

山有栲,	山上有栲树,
隰有杻。	洼地有杻树。
子有廷①内,	你有庭院和内室,
弗洒弗扫。	不洒水也不扫地。
子有钟鼓,	你有大钟和大鼓,
弗鼓弗考②。	不打也不敲。
宛其死矣,	要是一天死去了,
他人是保③。	别人一定来占有。
山有漆,	山上有漆树,
隰有栗。	洼地有栗树。
子有酒食,	你有酒和菜,
何不日鼓瑟?	何不每天弹琴瑟?
且以喜乐,	就这样求欢乐,
且以永日。	就这样度时日。
宛其死矣,	要是一天死去了,
他人入室。	别人一定进堂屋。

扬之水

扬之水,	舒缓不息的河水,
白石凿凿④。	河水中白石鲜明。

---

① 廷:庭院。
② 考:打击。
③ 保:占有。
④ 凿凿:鲜明的样子。

Uphill you've varnish trees;
Downhill trees rooted deep.
You have rooms as you please.
Why not clean them and sweep?
You have your drum and bell.
Why don't you beat and ring?
One day when tolls your knell,
Joy to others they'll bring.

Uphill you've chestnut trees;
Downhill trees with deep root.
You have wine as you please.
Why not play lyre and lute
To be cheerful and gay
And to prolong your bloom?
When you are dead one day,
Others will enter your room.

Our Prince[1]

The clear stream flows ahead
And the white rocks out stand.

---

[1] The prince referred to the uncle of Marquis Zhao of Jin, who was raised by a rebellious party to displace the Marquis in 73 B. C.. The rocks were symbolic of the conspirators and the speaker was an adherent of the conspiracy who had heard the secret order to conspire against Marquis Zhao of Jin.

素衣朱襮①,	身着素净的红领征衣,
从子于沃。	大家相送你到曲沃。
既见君子,	已经看到君子了,
云何不乐?	怎不心喜若狂?
扬之水,	舒缓不息的河水,
白石皓皓。	河水中白石皓洁。
素衣朱绣,	身着素净的红领征衣,
从子于鹄。	大家相送你到鹄邑。
既见君子,	已经看到君子了,
云何其忧?	又有何值得去忧伤?
扬之水,	舒缓不息的河水,
白石粼粼②。	河水中白石清澄。
我闻有命,	我听说将有命令,
不敢以告人。	如何敢把它告诉别人。

椒 聊 ③

椒聊之实,	串串花椒的种子,
蕃衍盈升。	繁多得超过一升。

---

① 襮(bó):绣有图案的衣领。
② 粼粼:清澈澄明的样子。
③ 椒聊:花椒的种子多成串。

In our plain dress with collars red,
We follow you to eastern land.
Shall we not rejoice since
We have seen our dear prince?

The clear stream flows ahead
And naked rocks out stand.
In plain dress with sleeves broidered red,
We follow you to northern land.
How can we feel sad since
We have seen our dear prince?

The clear stream flows along the border;
Wave-beaten rocks stand out.
We've heard the secret order,
But nothing should be talked about.

The Pepper Plant[①]

The fruit of pepper plant
Is so luxuriant.

[①] The productive pepper plant referred to a reproductive or fertile woman. That is the reason why a woman's bedroom was called pepper chamber in Chinese.

彼其之子，　　　　　　　那个人的儿子，
硕大无朋①。　　　　　　魁梧高大无人能比。
椒聊且！　　　　　　　　像一串串花椒啊！
远条②且！　　　　　　　香味悠远啊！

椒聊之实，　　　　　　　串串花椒的种子，
蕃衍盈匊③。　　　　　　繁多得超过一捧。
彼其之子，　　　　　　　那个妇人子孙多。
硕大且笃。　　　　　　　魁梧高大忠实敦厚。
椒聊且！　　　　　　　　像一串串花椒啊！
远条且！　　　　　　　　香味悠远啊！

绸　缪④

绸缪束薪，　　　　　　　捆好柴薪，
三星⑤在天。　　　　　　三星在天上。
今夕何夕，　　　　　　　今夜是什么日子，
见此良人？　　　　　　　能看到这个好人？
子兮子兮，　　　　　　　你啊你啊，
如此良人何？　　　　　　像你这样的好人该怎么办啊？

① 无朋：无比。
② 远条：长远，悠远。
③ 匊：两手合捧。
④ 绸缪：缠绵，捆好。
⑤ 三星：指参星。

The woman there
Is large beyond compare.
O pepper plant, extend
Your shoots without end!

The pepper plant there stands;
Its fruit will fill our hands.
The woman here
Is large without a peer.
O pepper plant, extend
Your shoots without end!

A Wedding Song[1]

The firewood's tightly bound
When in the sky three stars appear.
What evening's coming round
For me to find my bridegroom here!
O he is here! O he is here!
What shall I not do with my dear!

---

[1] The firewood or hay or thorns tightly bound alluded to husband and wife well united. The first stanza should be sung by the bride, the second by the guests and the third by the bridegroom.

绸缪束刍①,　　　　　　　　捆好青草,
三星在隅。　　　　　　　　三星在屋角。
今夕何夕,　　　　　　　　今夜是什么日子,
见此邂逅②?　　　　　　　能够不约而遇?
子兮子兮,　　　　　　　　你啊你啊,
如此邂逅何?　　　　　　　像这样不约而遇该怎么办啊?

绸缪束楚,　　　　　　　　捆好荆条,
三星在户。　　　　　　　　三星在门上。
今夕何夕,　　　　　　　　今夜是什么日子,
见此粲者③?　　　　　　　能看到这个美人?
子兮子兮,　　　　　　　　你啊你啊,
如此粲者何?　　　　　　　像你这样的美人该怎么办啊?

杕 杜

有杕之杜⑤,　　　　　　　孤独的赤棠,
其叶湑湑⑥。　　　　　　　叶子繁茂。
独行踽踽⑦,　　　　　　　孤独地行走,
岂无他人?　　　　　　　　难道没有别人?

---

① 刍:青草。
② 邂逅:不约而遇。
③ 粲者:指前面说的"良人"。
④ 杕(dì):特立的样子。
⑤ 杜:赤棠。
⑥ 湑湑(xǔ xǔ):繁茂的样子。
⑦ 踽踽:孤独的样子。

The hay is tightly bound
When o'er the house three stars appear.
What night is coming round
To find this couple here!
O they are here! O they are here!
How lucky to see this couple dear!

The thorns are tightly bound
When o'er the door three stars appear.
What midnight's coming round
For me to find my beauty here!
O she is here! O she is here!
What shall I not do with my dear?

A Wanderer[①]

A tree of russet pear
Has leaves so thickly grown.
Alone I wander there
With no friends of my own.
Is there no one
Who would of me take care?

---

① This was the lament of a beggar deprived of his brothers and relatives or forsaken by them.

不如我同父^①。	不像我同族的兄弟亲。
嗟行之人，	独行叹息的人，
胡不比^②焉？	为什么没有人做伴？
人无兄弟，	人要是没有兄弟，
胡不佽^③焉？	谁与他同甘共苦？

有杕之杜，	孤独的赤棠，
其叶菁菁。	叶子茂盛。
独行睘睘^④，	孤独地行走，
岂无他人？	难道没有别人？
不如我同姓。	不像我同族的兄弟亲。

嗟行之人，	独行叹息的人，
胡不比焉？	为什么没有人做伴？
人无兄弟，	人要是没有兄弟，
胡不佽焉？	谁与他同甘共苦？

① 同父：同一个祖父的兄弟。
② 比：辅助。
③ 佽（cì）：帮助。
④ 睘睘（qióng qióng）：孤独的样子。

But there is none
Like my own father's son.
O wanderer, why are there few
To sympathize with you?
Can you not find another
To help you like a brother?

A tree of russet pear
Has leaves so lushly grown.
Alone I loiter there
Without a kinsman of my own.
Is there no one
Who would take care of me?
But there is none
Like my own family.
O loiterer, why are there few
To sympathize with you?
Can you not find another
To help you like a brother?

羔 裘

羔裘豹袪①,　　　　　　　　羊皮袍子豹皮袖,
自我人居居②。　　　　　　　对人傲慢态度差。
岂无他人?　　　　　　　　　难道没有其他大人?
维子之故!　　　　　　　　　只是与你念及情谊!

羔裘豹褎③,　　　　　　　　羊皮袍子豹皮袖,
自我人究究。　　　　　　　　对人傲慢态度差。
岂无他人?　　　　　　　　　难道没有其他大人?
维子之好!　　　　　　　　　只是念及你我旧交!

鸨 羽

肃肃④鸨羽,　　　　　　　　鸨鸟展翅沙沙响,
集⑤于苞⑥栩。　　　　　　　停在丛生柞树上。
王事靡盬⑦,　　　　　　　　国王的差事无休止,
不能蓺⑧稷黍,　　　　　　　不能回家种稷黍,
父母何怙⑨?　　　　　　　　靠什么养活父母?
悠悠苍天!　　　　　　　　　悠远的苍天啊!
曷其有所?　　　　　　　　　什么时候才能回家乡?

① 袪(qū):袖子。
② 居居:同"倨倨",恶劣。
③ 褎(xiù):袖子。
④ 肃肃:鸨鸟展翅飞的声音。
⑤ 集:群鸟停歇在树上。
⑥ 苞:丛生。
⑦ 盬(gǔ):停歇。
⑧ 蓺(yì):种植。
⑨ 怙:依靠。

An Unkind Lord in Lamb's Fur[1]

Lamb's fur and leopard's cuff,
To us you are so rough.
Can't we find another chief
Who would cause us no grief?

Lamb's fur and leopard's cuff,
You ne'er give us enough.
Can't we find another chief
Who would assuage our grief?

The Peasants' Complaint[2]

Swish, swish sound the plumes of wild geese;
They can't alight on bushy trees.
We must discharge the king's affair.
How can we plant our millet with care?
On what can our parents rely?
O gods in boundless, endless sky,
When can we live in peace? I sigh.

---

[1] The people of some lord complained of his hard treatment of them.
[2] The men of Jin called out to warfare by the king's order mourned over the consequent suffering of their parents and longed for their return to their ordinary agricultural pursuits.

肃肃鸨翼，	鸨鸟展翅沙沙响，
集于苞棘。	停在丛生枣树上。
王事靡盬，	国王的差事做不完，
不能蓺黍稷，	不能回家种黍稷，
父母何食？	父母靠什么吃饭？
悠悠苍天！	悠远的苍天啊！
曷其有极？	什么时候才有能结束？

肃肃鸨行，	鸨鸟展翅沙沙响，
集于包桑。	停在丛生桑树上。
王事靡盬，	国王的差事做不完，
不能蓺稻粱，	不能回家种稻粱，
父母何尝？	父母用何去果腹？
悠悠苍天！	悠远的苍天啊！
曷其有常？	什么时候才能得安康？

无 衣

岂曰无衣七兮？	怎么说我没有七套衣裳？
不如子之衣，	只是不像你的衣裳，
安且吉兮！	舒适又漂亮！

岂曰无衣六兮？	怎么说我没有六套衣裳？
不如子之衣，	只是不像你的衣裳，
安且燠①兮！	舒服又暖和！

① 燠（yù）：暖和。

Swish, swish flap the wings of wild geese;
They can't alight on jujube trees.
We must discharge the king's affair.
How can we plant our maize with care?
On what can our parents live and rely?
O gods in boundless, endless sky,
Can all this end before I die?

Swish, swish come the rows of wild geese;
They can't alight on mulberries.
We must discharge the king's affair.
How can we plant our rice with care?
What can our parents have for food?
O Heaven good, O Heaven good!
When can we gain a livelihood?

To His Deceased Wife[①]

Have I no dress? You made me seven.
I'm comfortless,
Now you're in heaven.

Have I no dress? You made me six.
I'm comfortless
As if on pricks.

---

① The speaker was thinking of his deceased wife who had made his dress for him.

有杕之杜

有杕之杜，	一棵孤伶的赤棠，
生于道左。	长在路的左旁。
彼君子兮，	那个君子人啊，
噬①肯适我？	可会来到我这边？
中心好之，	心中那么喜欢他，
曷饮食之？	怎不备好酒菜款待他？

有杕之杜，	一棵孤伶的赤棠，
生于道周②。	长在路的右旁。
彼君子兮，	那个君子人啊，
噬肯来游？	可会逛到我这边？
中心好之，	心中那么喜欢他，
曷饮食之？	怎不备好酒菜款待他？

葛　生

葛生蒙③楚，	葛藤缠绕荆条，
蔹④蔓于野。	白蔹蔓延荒郊。
予美亡此，	我爱的人逝这里，
谁与独处！	谁让我一个人孤独自守！

---

① 噬：何，怎么。
② 周：右。
③ 蒙：覆盖。
④ 蔹（liǎn）：白蔹，一种植物，根可以药用。

The Russet Pear Tree[①]

A lonely tree of russet pear
Stands still on the left of the way.
O you for whom I care,
Won't you come as I pray?
In my heart you're so sweet.
When may I give you food to eat?

A lonely tree of russet pear
Stands still on the road's right-hand side.
O you for whom I care,
Won't you come for a ride?
In my heart you're so sweet.
When may I give you food to eat?

An Elegy[②]

Vine grows o'er the thorn tree;
Weeds in the field o'erspread.
The man I love is dead.
Who'd dwell alone with thee?

[①] The russet pear tree was said to be symbolic of a lonely woman longing for her lover.
[②] This was the first elegy in Chinese poetry. A widow mourned the death of her husband killed in the war waged by Duke Xian of Jin(reigned 675—650 B. C.). The vine supported by the tree might be suggestive of the widow's own desolate, unsupported condition or descriptive of the battleground where her husband had met his death.

葛生蒙棘，　　　　　　　　葛藤缠绕枣树，
蔹蔓于域①。　　　　　　　白蔹蔓延荒郊。
予美亡此，　　　　　　　　我爱的人逝这里，
谁与独息！　　　　　　　　谁让我一个人独自息睡！

角枕粲兮，　　　　　　　　牛角枕鲜明啊，
锦衾烂兮。　　　　　　　　锦绣被绚烂啊。
予美亡此，　　　　　　　　我爱的人逝这里，
谁与独旦！　　　　　　　　谁让我一个人独守到天亮。

夏之日，　　　　　　　　　夏天的日长，
冬之夜。　　　　　　　　　冬天的夜长。
百岁之后，　　　　　　　　百年以后，
归于其居②！　　　　　　　我要与他相会在坟场。

冬之夜，　　　　　　　　　冬天的夜长，
夏之日。　　　　　　　　　夏天的日长。
百岁之后，　　　　　　　　百年以后，
归于其室③！　　　　　　　我要去他墓中相依傍！

采 苓④

采苓采苓，　　　　　　　　采甘草啊采甘草，
首阳之颠。　　　　　　　　在首阳山顶找。

① 域：坟地。
② 居：坟墓。
③ 室：坟坑。
④ 苓：甘草。

Vine grows o'er jujube tree;
Weeds o'er the graveyard spread.
The man I love is dead.
Who'd stay alone with thee?

How fair the pillow of horn
And the embroidered bed!
The man I love is dead.
Who'd stay with thee till morn?

Long is the summer day;
Cold winter night appears.
After a hundred years
In the same tomb we'd stay.

The winter night is cold;
Long is the summer day.
When I have passed away.
We'll be in same household.

Rumor[①]

Could the sweet water plant be found
On the top of the mountain high?

[①] This was directed against Duke Xian of Jin who killed his son on believing rumors. Rumors should no more be believed than water plants could be found on the top of the mountain.

人之为①言，　　　　　　　别人说的假话，
苟②亦无信。　　　　　　　真的不要相信。
舍旃舍旃③，　　　　　　　放弃它放弃它，
苟亦无然。　　　　　　　　那些全都不可靠。
人之为言，　　　　　　　　别人的话，
胡得焉！　　　　　　　　　能得到什么呢！

采苦采苦，　　　　　　　　采苦菜啊采苦菜，
首阳之下。　　　　　　　　在首阳山下找。
人之为言，　　　　　　　　别人说的假话，
苟亦无与④。　　　　　　　真的不要赞同。
舍旃舍旃，　　　　　　　　放弃它放弃它，
苟亦无然。　　　　　　　　那些全都不可靠。
人之为言，　　　　　　　　别人的话，
胡得焉！　　　　　　　　　能得到什么呢！

采葑采葑，　　　　　　　　采芜菁啊采芜菁，
首阳之东。　　　　　　　　在首阳山东找。
人⑤之为言，　　　　　　　别人说的假话，
苟亦无从。　　　　　　　　真的不要听从。
舍旃舍旃，　　　　　　　　放弃它放弃它，
苟亦无然。　　　　　　　　那些全都不可靠。
人之为言，　　　　　　　　别人的话，
胡得焉！　　　　　　　　　能得到什么呢！

① 为：即"伪"，假的。
② 苟：真的。
③ 旃：之，代指假话。
④ 与：理会。
⑤ 人：听从。

The rumor going round,
If not believed can't fly.
Put it aside, put it aside
So that it can't prevail.
The rumor spreading far and wide
Will be of no avail.

Could bitter water plant be found
At the foot of the mountain high?
The rumor going round
Is what we should deny.
Put it aside, put it aside
So that it can't prevail.
The rumor spreading far and wide
Will be of no avail.

Could water plants be found
East of the mountain high?
The rumor going round,
If disregarded, will die.
Put it aside, put it aside
So that it can't prevail.
The rumor spreading far and wide
Will be of no avail.

秦 风

车 邻

有车邻邻①,　　　　　　　　有车走过响辚辚,
有马白颠,　　　　　　　　　有马额顶是白色。
未见君子,　　　　　　　　　没有看见君子人,
寺人②之令。　　　　　　　　只是宦官传命令。

阪有漆,　　　　　　　　　　山坡种漆树,
隰有栗。　　　　　　　　　　洼地种栗树。
既见君子,　　　　　　　　　已经见到君子人,
并坐鼓瑟。　　　　　　　　　和他并坐来弹瑟。
"今者不乐,　　　　　　　　"今天不及时行乐,
逝者其耋③!"　　　　　　　　转眼就会变老翁!"

阪有桑,　　　　　　　　　　山坡种桑树,
隰有杨。　　　　　　　　　　洼地种杨树。
既见君子,　　　　　　　　　已经见到君子人,
并坐鼓簧。　　　　　　　　　和他并坐吹笙簧。
"今者不乐,　　　　　　　　"今天不及时行乐,
逝者其亡!"　　　　　　　　　转眼就会死去!"

---

① 邻邻:辚辚声。
② 寺人:宦官。
③ 耋:八十岁。

Songs Collected in Qin, Modern Shaanxi

Lord Zhong of Qin[①]

The cab bells ring;
Dappled steeds neigh.
"Let ushers bring
In friends so gay!"

There're varnish trees uphill
And chestnuts in lowland.
Friends see Lord Zhong sit still
Beside lute-playing band.
"If we do not enjoy today,
At eighty joy will pass away."

There're mulberries uphill
And willows in lowland.
Friends see Lord Zhong sit still
Beside his music band.
"If we do not enjoy today,
We'll regret when life ebbs away."

---

① This song celebrated the pleasures of Lord Zhong of Qin, who, made a great officer of the court by King Xuan in 826 B. C., began to turn Qin from a barbarian state to a music-loving civilized one, which unified China and founded the Empire of Qin in 221 B. C.

驷驖[1]

驷驖孔阜[2],　　　　　　　　四匹肥马毛色黑,
六辔在手。　　　　　　　　六根缰绳握在手。
公子媚子[3],　　　　　　　　公爷宠爱的那人,
从公于狩。　　　　　　　　跟从公爷去打猎。

奉[4]时辰牡[5],　　　　　　　供奉应时的野兽,
辰牡孔硕。　　　　　　　　肥大的野兽到处有。
公曰左之,　　　　　　　　公爷命令车向左,
舍拔[6]则获。　　　　　　　一箭射中那猎物。

游于北园,　　　　　　　　游猎在北园,
四马既闲。　　　　　　　　四马驾车很熟练。
輶[7]车鸾镳[8],　　　　　　　轻车鸾铃马衔镳,
载猃[9]歇骄[10]。　　　　　　众多猎狗车马间。

[1] 驷驖(tiě):四匹黑马。
[2] 阜:肥大。
[3] 媚子:宠爱的人。
[4] 奉:供奉,敬献。
[5] 辰牡:应时的公兽。
[6] 舍拔:射箭。
[7] 輶(yóu)车:轻车。
[8] 镳(biāo):马铁口。
[9] 猃(xiǎn):长嘴猎狗。
[10] 歇骄:短嘴猎狗。

Winter Hunting[1]

Holding in hand six reins
Of four iron-black steeds,
Our lord hunts on the plains
With good hunters he leads.

The male and female preys
Have grown to sizes fit.
"Shoot at the left!" he says;
Their arrows go and hit.

He comes to northern park
With his four steeds at leisure;
Long and short-mouthed hounds bark
In the carriage of pleasure.

---

[1] This song celebrated the growing opulence of Duke Xiang, grandson of Lord Zhong of Qin, as seen in his hunting in 769 B. C.

小 戎[①]

小戎伐[②]收，　　　　　　　小兵车又小车厢，
五楘[③]梁辀[④]。　　　　　　五皮革穿铜环绕车毂。
游环胁驱[⑤]，　　　　　　　活动的环圈控制骖马，
阴靷[⑥]鋈[⑦]续。　　　　　　革带穿铜环使骖马就范。
文茵[⑧]畅[⑨]毂[⑩]，　　　　虎皮垫铺在长毂车上，
驾我骐[⑪]馵[⑫]。　　　　　　驾车的青马后腿白色。
言念君子，　　　　　　　　　我想念那君子人啊，
温其如玉。　　　　　　　　　温和得像玉一样。
在其板屋，　　　　　　　　　他从军住在板木屋，
乱我心曲。　　　　　　　　　想他想得我心里乱。

四牡孔阜，　　　　　　　　　四匹雄马真肥大，
六辔在手。　　　　　　　　　六根缰绳拿在手。
骐骝[⑬]是中，　　　　　　　两匹赤身黑鬣的服马在中间，
騧[⑭]骊是骖。　　　　　　　两匹黄身黑嘴的骖马在两边。

① 小戎：小兵车。
② 伐（jiàn）：浅。
③ 五楘（mù）：五束连络的皮革。
④ 梁辀（zhōu）：弯曲如船的车辕。
⑤ 胁驱：驾马的用具。
⑥ 阴靷（yǐn）：系骖马的革带。
⑦ 鋈（wù）：白铜环。
⑧ 文茵：虎皮垫。
⑨ 畅：长。
⑩ 毂（gǔ）：车轮中的圆木，中有圆孔，可以插轴。
⑪ 骐：青黑色的马。
⑫ 馵（zhù）：左后足白色的马。
⑬ 骝（liú）：赤身黑鬣的马。
⑭ 騧（guā）：黄身黑嘴的马。

A Lord on Expedition[①]

His chariot finely bound,
Crisscrossed with straps around,
Covered with tiger's skin,
Driven by horses twin;
His steeds controlled with reins
Through slip rings like gilt chains;
I think of my lord dear
Far-off on the frontier;
He's pure as jade and plain.
O my heart throbs with pain.

His four fine steeds there stand;
He holds six reins in hand.
The insides have black mane,
Yellow the outside twain.

---

① The wife of a Qin lord absent on an expedition against the western tribes who killed King You of Zhou in 771 B. C., gave a glowing description of his chariot, steeds and weapons and expressed her regret at his absence.

龙盾①之合, 画龙的盾牌双双合在车前面,
鋈以觼軜②。 银环把骖马的内缰绳来串联。
言念君子, 我想念的那君子人啊,
温其在邑。 温和在邑可以为友。
方何为期, 什么时候才能回来啊,
胡然我念之。 叫我怎么不想他啊。

伐驷③孔群④, 薄金甲的四匹马多威风,
厹矛⑤鋈錞⑥。 三隅矛杆下装着白银錞。
蒙伐⑦有苑⑧, 盾牌上画着鸟羽纹,
虎韔⑨镂膺⑩。 刻金的虎皮弓囊雕刻纹。
交韔二弓, 两弓交错在弓囊中,
竹闭⑪绲⑫縢⑬。 竹制弓檠绳索捆。
言念君子, 我想念那君子人啊,
载寝载兴。 早起晚睡不安宁。
厌厌⑭良人, 那温良文静的人啊,
秩秩德音。 明慧有礼贤德行。

① 龙盾:画有龙形的盾。
② 觼軜(jué nà):有舌环穿过骖马的皮带,使内辔固定。
③ 伐驷:披薄金甲的四匹马。
④ 孔群:很合群。
⑤ 厹(qiú)矛:三棱锋刃的矛。
⑥ 鋈錞(wù duì):用白铜镀矛柄底的金属套。
⑦ 伐:盾牌。
⑧ 苑:文彩。
⑨ 虎韔(chàng):用虎皮做的弓囊。
⑩ 镂膺:刻纹。
⑪ 闭:弓檠。
⑫ 绲(gǔn):绳。
⑬ 縢:缠束。
⑭ 厌厌:安静的样子。

Dragon shields on two wings,
Buckled up as with strings.
I think of my lord dear
So good on the frontier.
When will he come to me?
Can I be yearning-free?

How fine his team appears!
How bright his trident spears!
His shield bears a carved face;
In tiger's skin bow-case
With bamboo frames and bound
With strings, two bows are found.
I think of my dear mate,
Rise early and sleep late.
My dear, dear one,
Can I forget the good you've done?

蒹 葭[①]

蒹葭苍苍，　　　　　　　　初生的芦苇色青苍，
白露为霜。　　　　　　　　夜来白露凝成霜。
所谓伊人，　　　　　　　　所说的那个人，
在水一方。　　　　　　　　在水的那一方。
溯洄[②]从之，　　　　　　　逆水而上去找她，
道阻且长；　　　　　　　　道路崎岖长又长；
溯游[③]从之，　　　　　　　顺流而下去寻她，
宛在水中央。　　　　　　　仿佛在那水中央。

蒹葭萋萋，　　　　　　　　芦苇长得很茂盛，
白露未晞[④]。　　　　　　　路上白露还未干。
所谓伊人，　　　　　　　　所说的那个人，
在水之湄[⑤]。　　　　　　　在那水草滩。
溯洄从之，　　　　　　　　逆水而上去找她，
道阻且跻；　　　　　　　　道路崎岖难攀登；
溯游从之，　　　　　　　　顺流而下去寻她，
宛在水中坻[⑥]。　　　　　　仿佛在那水中沙滩。

蒹葭采采，　　　　　　　　芦苇长得连成片，
白露未已。　　　　　　　　路上白露没有干。

① 蒹葭：初生的芦苇。
② 溯洄：逆流而上。
③ 溯游：顺流而下。
④ 晞：干。
⑤ 湄：水草相关的地方。
⑥ 坻：水中的小高地。

Where Is She?[1]

Green, green the reed,
Frost and dew gleam
Where's she I need?
Beyond the stream.
Upstream I go;
The way's so long.
And downstream, lo!
She's thereamong.

White, white the reed,
Dew not yet dried.
Where's she I need?
On the other side.
Upstream I go;
Hard is the way.
And downstream, lo!
She's far away.

Bright, bright the reed,
With frost dews blend.

---

[1] This was said to be the first symbolic love song in Chinese poetry.

所谓伊人,　　　　　　　　　所说的那个人,
在水之涘①。　　　　　　　　在水的那一岸。
溯洄从之,　　　　　　　　　逆水而上去找她,
道阻且右;　　　　　　　　　道路崎岖弯又弯;
溯游从之,　　　　　　　　　顺流而下去寻她,
宛在水中沚②。　　　　　　　仿佛在那水中小洲。

终 南

终南何有?　　　　　　　　　终南山上长什么?
有条③有梅。　　　　　　　　有山楸树有红梅。
君子至止,　　　　　　　　　君子来到这里住,
锦衣狐裘。　　　　　　　　　穿着锦衣和狐裘。
颜如渥丹,　　　　　　　　　面目丰满又红润,
其君也哉!　　　　　　　　　真是尊贵好君王!

终南何有?　　　　　　　　　终南山上长什么?
有纪④有堂⑤。　　　　　　　有杞树又有赤棠。
君子至止,　　　　　　　　　君子来到这里住,
黻⑥衣绣裳。　　　　　　　　穿着锦衣和绣裳。
佩玉将将,　　　　　　　　　佩带美玉响叮响,
寿考不忘!　　　　　　　　　祝你长寿永安康!

① 涘(sì):水边。
② 沚(zhǐ):水中的沙洲。
③ 条:小楸树。
④ 纪:杞树。
⑤ 堂:赤棠树。
⑥ 黻(fú):绣着青黑色。

Where's she I need?
At river's end.
Upstream I go;
The way does wind.
And downstream, lo!
She's far behind.

Duke Xiang of Qin[①]

What's on the southern hill?
There're mume trees and white firs.
Our lord comes and stands still,
Wearing a robe and furs.
Vermillion is his face.
O what majestic grace!

What's on the southern hill?
There are trees of white pears.
Our lord comes and stands still;
A broidered robe he wears.
His gems give tinkling sound.
Long live our lord black-gowned!

[①] This song celebrated the dignity of Duke Xiang of Qin, the first of Qin lords recognized as a prince of the kingdom, who, wearing the black ducal robe conferred by King Ping in 769 B. C. after his victory over the western tribes who had killed King You in 771 B. C., passed by the Southern Mountain 25 killometres south of the capital (modern Xi'an) on his homeward way to Qin.

黄 鸟

交交①黄鸟，	黄鸟交交叫，
止于棘。	停在枣树上。
谁从②穆公?	谁从穆公去陪葬?
子车奄息。	子车氏叫奄息的人。
维此奄息，	这个奄息，
百夫之特③。	才德百人比不上。
临其穴，	走近他的墓穴，
惴惴其栗。	浑身战栗心里慌。
彼苍者天，	那苍天啊，
歼④我良人!	杀我的好人!
如可赎兮，	如果可以赎他的命啊，
人百其身!	人愿意死百次来抵偿!
交交黄鸟，	黄鸟交交叫，
止于桑。	停在桑树上。
谁从穆公?	谁从穆公去陪葬?
子车仲行。	子车氏叫仲行的人。
维此仲行，	这个仲行，
百夫之防⑤。	才德百人难能比。

① 交交：黄鸟鸣叫的声音。
② 从：从死，陪葬。
③ 特：杰出。
④ 歼：灭亡，杀害。
⑤ 防：抵当。

Burial of Three Worthies[1]

The golden orioles flew
And lit on jujube tree.
Who's buried with Duke Mu?
The eldest of the three.
This eldest worthy son
Could be rivaled by none.
Coming to the graveside,
Who'd not be terrified?
O good Heavens on high,
Why should the worthy die?
If he could live again,
Who not have been slain?

The golden oriole flew
And lit on mulberry.
Who's buried with Duke Mu?
The second of the three.
The second worthy son
Could be equalled by none.

---

[1] The three worthies were buried alive together with 174 others in the same grave with Duke Mu of Qin in 620 B. C. They were not so free as the golden oriole.

临其穴,	走近他的墓穴,
惴惴其栗。	浑身战栗心里慌。
彼苍者天,	那苍天啊,
歼我良人!	杀我的好人!
如可赎兮,	如果可以赎他的命啊,
人百其身!	人愿意死百次来抵偿!

交交黄鸟,	黄鸟交交叫,
止于楚。	停在荆条上。
谁从穆公?	谁从穆公去陪葬?
子车铖虎。	子车氏叫铖虎的人。
维此铖虎,	这个铖虎,
百夫之御①。	才德百人没他强。
临其穴,	走近他的墓穴,
惴惴其栗。	浑身战栗心里慌。
彼苍者天,	那苍天啊,
歼我良人!	杀我的好人!
如可赎兮,	如果可以赎他的命啊,
人百其身!	人愿意死百次来抵偿!

晨 风②

鴥③彼晨风,	晨风鸟飞得急,
郁彼北林。	北林树长得密。

---

① 御:抵挡。
② 晨风:鸟名。
③ 鴥(yù):鸟儿疾飞的样子。

Coming to the graveside,
Who'd not be terrified?
O good Heavens on high,
Why should the worthy die?
If he could live again,
Who would not have been slain?

The golden oriole flew
And lit on the thorn tree.
Who's buried with Duke Mu?
The youngest of the three.
The youngest worthy son
Could be surpassed by none.
Coming to the graveside,
Who'd not be terrified?
O good Heavens on high,
Why should the worthy die?
If he could live again,
Who would not have been slain?

The Forgotten[①]

The falcon flies above
To the thick northern wood.

[①] A wife told her grief because of the absence of her husband and his forgetfulness of her.

未见君子,	没有见到君子人,
忧心钦钦①。	我的心里多忧伤。
如何如何?	为什么啊为什么?
忘我实多!	把我忘得无踪影!

山有苞栎,	山上栎树丛生,
隰有六驳。	洼地多长榆树。
未见君子,	没有见到君子人,
忧心靡乐。	我的心里不快乐。
如何如何?	为什么啊为什么?
忘我实多!	把我忘得无踪影!

山有苞棣,	山上郁李丛生,
隰有树檖。	洼地长着山梨。
未见君子,	没有见到君子人,
忧心如醉,	我的心里如酒醉。
如何如何?	为什么啊为什么?
忘我实多!	把我忘得无踪影!

无 衣

岂曰无衣?	谁说没有衣服穿?
与子同袍。	你与我同穿长袍。

① 钦钦:忧愁的样子。

While I see not my love,
I'm in a gloomy mood.
How can it be my lot
To be so much forgot?

The bushy oaks above
And six elm-trees below.
While I see not my love,
There is no joy I know.
How can it be my lot
To be so much forgot?

The sparrow-plums above
Below trees without leaf.
While I see not my love,
My heart is drunk with grief.
How can it be my lot
To be so much forgot?

Comradeship[1]

Are you not battle-drest?
Let's share the plate for breast!

---

[1] This was the song sung by Duke Ai of Qin when he despatched five hundred chariots to the rescue of the State of Chu besieged by Wu in 505 B. C.

王于兴师，	国王要起兵，
修我戈矛，	修理我的戈与矛，
与子同仇。	与你同对仇人。 |//

岂曰无衣？	谁说没有衣服穿？
与子同泽[①]。	你与我同穿汗衫。
王于兴师，	国王要起兵，
修我矛戟，	修理我的矛与戟，
与子偕作！	与你一起作战。

岂曰无衣？	谁说没有衣服穿？
与子同裳。	你我同穿战裙。
王于兴师，	国王要起兵，
修我甲兵，	修理我的盔甲和刀枪，
与子偕行！	与你一起前行。

渭　阳

我送舅氏，	我给舅舅送行，
曰至渭阳。	送到渭水的北边。
何以赠之？	拿什么送给他？
路车乘黄。	黄马大车表我心。

① 泽：贴身穿的汗衫。

We shall go up the line.
Let's make our lances shine!
Your foe is mine.

Are you not battle-drest?
Let's share the coat and vest!
We shall go up the line.
Let's make our halberds shine!
Your job is mine.

Are you not battle-drest?
Let's share the kilt and the rest!
We shall go up the line.
Let's make our armour shine!
We'll march your hand in mine.

Farewell to Duke Wen of Jin[①]

I see my uncle dear
Off north of River Wei.
What's the gift for one I revere?
Golden cab on the way.

---

① This song was sung by Duke Kang of Qin in 635 B. C. while, heir-apparent of Qin, he escorted his uncle into the State of Jin where he became the famous Duke Wen after nineteen years' refuge in Qin.

我送舅氏，	我给舅舅送行，
悠悠我思①。	想念我的娘亲。
何以赠之？	拿什么送给他？
琼瑰②玉佩。	美玉琼瑶表我心。

权　舆

於！我乎，	唉！我啊，
夏屋③渠渠④，	当初大碗盛得满，
今也每食无余。	现在每顿都吃光。
于嗟乎！	唉呀！
不承权舆⑤！	不能去跟当初比啊！

於！我乎，	唉！我啊，
每食四簋⑥，	当初每顿四大盆，
今也每食不饱，	现在每顿填不饱。
于嗟呼！	唉呀！
不承权舆！	不能去跟当初比啊！

---

① 悠悠我思：指思念母亲。
② 琼瑰：美玉。
③ 夏屋：一种大的食器。
④ 渠渠：盛，满。
⑤ 权舆：当初，开始的时候。
⑥ 簋：一种食器。

I see my uncle dear
Off and think of my mother.
What's the gift for one she and I revere?
Jewels and gems for her brother.

Not As Before[1]

Ah me! Where is my house of yore?
Now I've not a great deal
To eat at every meal.
Alas!
I can't live as before.

Ah me!
Where are my dishes four?
Now hungry I feel at every meal.
Alas!
I can't eat as before.

---

[1] This song was said to be a complaint against Duke Kang of Qin who was not so hospitable as Lord Zhong (in Poem "Lord Zhong of Qin") and Duke Mu of Qin.

陈 风

宛 丘

子之汤①兮，	你的舞姿飘荡啊，
宛丘②之上兮。	在宛丘的上面啊。
洵有情兮，	我诚有深情啊，
而无望③兮。	却徒然无望啊。

坎其击鼓，	咚咚咚把鼓敲响，
宛丘之下。	在宛丘的下面啊。
无冬无夏，	不分冬夏舞不停，
值④其鹭羽。	摇着鹭鸶的羽毛。

坎其击缶，	当当当把缶敲响，
宛丘之道。	在宛丘的路上啊。
无冬无夏，	不分冬夏舞不停，
值其鹭翿⑤。	舞着鹭鸶的羽毛。

① 汤：即"荡"，飘荡。
② 宛丘：四边高、中间低的土山。
③ 望：指望，盼头。
④ 值：持，拿着。
⑤ 翿（dào）：一种带羽毛的舞具。

Songs Collected in Chen, Modern Henan

A Religious Dancer[1]

In the highland above
A witch dances with swing.
With her I fall in love;
Hopeless, I sing.

She beats the drum
At the foot of highland.
Winter and summer come,
She dances plume in hand.

She beats a vessel round
On the way to highland.
Spring or fall comes around,
She dances fan in hand.

[1] This song described the pleasure-seeking of the people of Chen in the capital where there was a mound in the highland, favorite resort of pleasure-seekers.

东门之枌[1]

东门之枌, 东门外的白榆树,
宛丘之栩[2]。 宛丘上的柞树。
子仲之子, 子仲家的姑娘,
婆娑[3]其下。 大树下起舞。

穀旦[4]于差[5], 选择一个好日子,
南方之原。 去到南边的平原上。
不绩其麻, 不纺手中麻,
市也婆娑。 闹市舞一场。

穀旦于逝, 大好时光要结束,
越以鬷[6]迈。 你我屡屡总相遇。
视尔如荍[7], 看你美如荆葵花,
贻我握椒。 送我一束香花椒。

衡 门

衡门之下, 支起横木即是门,
可以栖迟。 横木之下来栖身。

---

[1] 枌(fén):白榆树。
[2] 栩:柞树。
[3] 婆娑:舞蹈。
[4] 穀旦:好日子。
[5] 差:选择。
[6] 鬷(zōng):总,屡次。
[7] 荍(qiáo):荆葵。

Secular Dancers[1]

From white elms at east gate
To oak-trees on the mound
Lad and lass have a date;
They dance gaily around.

A good morning is chosen
To go to the south where,
Leaving the hemp unwoven,
They dance at country fair.

They go at morning hours
Together to highland.
Lasses look like sunflowers,
A token of love in hand.

Contentment[2]

Beneath the door of single beam
You can sit and rest at your leisure;

---

[1] This song described wanton associations of the young people of Chen. The mound at the eastern gate was a favorite resort of pleasure-seekers.
[2] This showed that one might enjoy oneself and forget one's hunger, be satisfied with fish of smaller note and be happy with a wife though she were not of a noble family.

泌之洋洋，
可以乐饥①。

泌水荡漾漾，
快乐慰饥肠。

岂其食鱼，
必河之鲂？
岂其取妻，
必齐之姜？

难道想要吃鱼，
一定要吃黄河里的鳊鱼？
难道想要娶妻，
一定要娶齐国姜家女？

岂其食鱼，
必河之鲤？
岂其取妻，
必宋之子？

难道吃鱼，
一定要吃黄河里的鲤鱼？
难道想要娶妻，
一定要娶宋国子家大姑娘？

东门之池

东门之池，
可以沤②麻。
彼美淑姬，
可与晤歌。

东门外的池塘，
可以沤麻制衣裳。
端庄美丽的姑娘，
可以和她对唱。

东门之池，
可以沤纻③。
彼美淑姬，
可与晤语。

东门外的池塘，
可以沤纻做衣裳。
端庄美丽的姑娘，
可以和她倾情肠。

① 乐饥：乐而忘饥。
② 沤：长时间泡。
③ 纻：苎麻。

Beside the gently flowing stream
You may drink to stay hunger with pleasure.

If you want to eat fish,
Why must you have bream as you wish?
If you want to be wed,
Why must you have Qi the nobly bred?

If you want to eat fish,
Why must you have carp as you wish?
If you want to be wed,
Why must you have Song the highly bred?

To a Weaving Maiden[①]

At eastern gate we could
Steep hemp in river long.
O maiden fair and good,
To you I'll sing a song.

At eastern gate we could
Steep nettle in the creek.
O maiden fair and good,
To you I wish to speak.

---

① The stalks of the hemp had to be steeped, preparatory to getting the threads or filaments from them so that the maiden might weave clothes.

东门之池,	东门外的池塘,
可以沤菅①。	可以沤菅。
彼美淑姬,	端庄美丽的姑娘,
可与晤言。	和她叙话心花放。

东门之杨

东门之杨,	东门外的杨树,
其叶牂牂②。	叶子沙沙响。
昏以为期,	约定在黄昏的时候,
明星煌煌。	长庚星闪闪发光。

东门之杨,	东门外的杨树,
其叶肺肺③。	叶子哗哗响。
昏以为期,	约定在黄昏的时候,
明星晢晢④。	长庚星发光灼灼。

墓 门

墓门有棘,	墓门旁边有枣树,
斧以斯⑤之。	挥动斧头把它砍。

---

① 菅：菅草。
② 牂牂（zāng zāng）：风吹树叶的声音。
③ 肺肺：同"牂牂"。
④ 晢晢（zhé zhé）：明亮的样子。
⑤ 斯：砍掉。

At eastern gate we could
Steep in the moat rush-rope.
O maiden fair and good,
On you I hang my hope.

A Date[1]

On poplars by east gate
The leaves are rustling light.
At dusk we have a date;
The evening star shines bright.

On poplars by east gate
The leaves are shivering.
At dusk we have a date;
The morning star is quivering.

The Evil-Doing Usurper[2]

The thorn at burial gate
Should soon be cut away;

---

[1] The rustling poplar leaves and the evening star hinted at the lovers before their love-making and the shivering leaves and the morning star at the couple after their love-making.

[2] This was a satirical song directed against Tuo of Chen, a brother of Duke Huan (743—706 B. C.), upon whose death Tuo killed his eldest son and got possession of the State of Chen, but was killed by its neighboring State the year after. The thorn and the owl were both things of evil omen, and were employed here to introduce the evil-doing usurper. The legend went that this song was sung by a mulberry-gathering woman to ward off an official's attempt to rape her.

夫也不良，	那人不是好东西，
国人知之。	全国的人都知道。
知而不已，	知道他坏还不改，
谁昔①然矣！	由来已久这样坏！

墓门有梅，	墓门旁有酸梅树，
有鸮②萃③止。	猫头鹰来栖上面。
夫也不良，	那人不是好东西，
歌以讯④之。	想用作歌劝谏他。
讯予不顾，	劝谏他也不愿改，
颠倒思予！	是非好歹也不分！

防⑤有鹊巢

防有鹊巢，	堤岸上怎么会有鹊巢，
邛⑥有旨苕⑦。	山丘上怎么会有水草。
谁侜⑧予美，	谁在欺骗我的爱人，
心焉忉忉⑨。	我的心里很苦恼。

① 谁昔：即"畴昔"，从前。
② 鸮：猫头鹰。
③ 萃：集。
④ 讯：即"谇"，劝谏。
⑤ 防：堤岸。
⑥ 邛（qióng）：山丘。
⑦ 苕：水草。
⑧ 侜（zhōu）：欺骗。
⑨ 忉忉（dāo dāo）：苦恼。

The usurper of the State
Should be exposed to the day;
If he's exposed too late,
He'll still do what he may.

At burial gate there's jujube tree,
On which owls perch all the day long;
The usurper from evil is not free.
Let's warn him by a song!
But he won't listen to our plea,
For he takes right for wrong.

Riverside Magpies[1]

By riverside magpies appear;
On hillock water grasses grow.
Believe none who deceives, my dear,
Or my heart will be full of woe.

---

[1] This song might speak of the separation between lovers effected by evil tongues or refer to Duke Xuan of Chen (691—647 B. C.) who believed slanderers.

中唐①有甓②,　　　　　　　庭道上怎么会有瓦片,
邛有旨鹝③。　　　　　　　山丘上怎么会有水草。
谁侜予美,　　　　　　　　谁在欺骗我的爱人,
心焉惕惕。　　　　　　　　我的心里真烦恼。

月　出

月出皎④兮,　　　　　　　月儿出来明亮亮啊,
佼⑤人僚兮。　　　　　　　照着美人多漂亮啊。
舒窈纠⑥兮,　　　　　　　安闲的步子娇窕的影啊,
劳心悄⑦兮。　　　　　　　我的心儿多忧伤。

月出皓兮,　　　　　　　　月儿出来皓亮亮啊,
佼人懰⑧兮。　　　　　　　照着美人多俏丽啊。
舒忧受⑨兮,　　　　　　　安闲的步子婀娜的啊,
劳心慅⑩兮。　　　　　　　我的心儿多伤感啊。

月出照兮,　　　　　　　　月儿出来高高照啊,
佼人燎兮。　　　　　　　　照着美人多鲜亮啊。

① 唐:朝庭前的大路。
② 甓(pì):砖瓦。
③ 鹝(yì):绶草。
④ 皎:洁白明亮。
⑤ 佼:美好。
⑥ 窈纠(jiǎo):身姿苗条,行步舒缓的样子。
⑦ 悄:深忧烦恼。
⑧ 懰(liú):娇美。
⑨ 忧受:从容不迫,婀娜多姿的样子。
⑩ 慅(cǎo):忧愁的样子。

How can the court be paved with tiles
Or hillock spread with water grass?
Believe, my dear, none who beguiles,
Or I'll worry for you, alas!

The Moon[1]

The moon shines bright;
My love's snow-white.
She looks so cute.
Can I be mute?

The bright moon gleams;
My dear love beams.
Her face so fair,
Can I not care?

The bright moon turns;
With love she burns.

---

[1] This was the first song in Chinese poetry describing the poet's love for a beauty in moonlight.

舒夭绍①兮,	安闲的步子轻盈的行啊,
劳心惨兮。	我的心儿多忧愁啊。

株 林②

胡为乎株林?	为什么去株林?
从夏南③!	去找夏南!
匪适株林,	其实不是去株林,
从夏南!	是为了找夏南!
驾我乘马,	骑上我的大马,
说于株野。	在株林停下。
乘我乘驹,	骑上我的骏马,
朝食于株。	赶到株林食早饭。

泽 陂④

彼泽之陂,	那池塘的堤岸,
有蒲与荷。	长有蒲草伴荷花。
有美一人,	有一个美人儿,
伤如之何!	忧伤得怎么办!

---

① 夭绍:体态轻盈柔美的样子。
② 株林:夏姬的住处。
③ 夏南:夏姬的儿子。表面上说是看夏南,其实是看夏姬。
④ 陂(bēi):堤岸。

Her hands so fine,
Can I not pine?

The Duke's Mistress[①]

"Why are you going to the Wood?
To see the fair lady's son?"
"I'm going to its neighborhood
To see the son of the fair one.

"I'll drive to the countryside
And take a short rest there;
I'll change my horse and ride
To breakfast with the fair."

A Bewitching Lady[②]

By poolside over there
Grow reed and lotus bloom.
There is a lady fair
Whose heart is full of gloom.

---

① This song was directed against the intrigue of Duke Ling of Chen (reigned 612—598 B. C.) with the beautiful Lady Xia. The duke went to the wood in the countryside to tryst with her under the pretext of visiting her son Xia Nan, by whom he was killed in 598 B. C.
② It was said that this song described the bewitching Lady Xia mourning over the death of Duke Ling of Chen and her son Xia Nan killed by King Zhuang of Chu in 598 B. C. (See Poem "The Duke's Mistress").

寤寐①无为,　　　　　　　日夜相思没办法,
涕泗滂沱。　　　　　　　眼泪鼻涕一把把。

彼泽之陂,　　　　　　　那池塘的堤岸,
有蒲与蕑②。　　　　　　长有蒲草伴莲花。
有美一人,　　　　　　　有一个美人儿,
硕大且卷③。　　　　　　身材高大发饰美。
寤寐无为,　　　　　　　日夜相思没办法,
中心悁悁④。　　　　　　心中忧郁难打发。

彼泽之陂,　　　　　　　那池塘的堤岸,
有蒲菡萏⑤。　　　　　　长有蒲草伴荷花。
有美一人,　　　　　　　有一个美人儿,
硕大且俨。　　　　　　　身材高大貌端庄。
寤寐无为,　　　　　　　日夜相思没办法,
辗转伏枕。　　　　　　　翻来覆去空烦恼。

① 寤寐：醒着和睡着。
② 蕑（jiān）：莲。
③ 卷（quán）：即"鬈"，发饰美。
④ 悁悁（yuān yuān）：忧郁的样子。
⑤ 菡萏：荷花。

She does nothing in bed;
Like streams her tears are shed.

By poolside over there
Grow reed and orchid bloom.
There is a lady fair
Heart-broken, full of gloom.
Tall and with a curled head,
She does nothing in bed.

By poolside over there
Grow reed and lotus thin.
There is a lady fair
Tall and with double chin.
She does nothing in bed,
Tossing about her head.

桧　风

羔　裘

羔裘逍遥，	游玩时穿着羔裘，
狐裘以朝。	公堂上穿着狐裘。
岂不尔思？	难道我不想你吗？
劳心忉忉。	想你想得我心伤。
羔裘翱翔，	游逛时穿着羔裘，
狐裘在堂。	朝堂上穿着狐裘。
岂不尔思？	难道我不想你吗？
我心忧伤。	担心国事我忧伤。
羔裘如膏，	羔裘如膏脂润泽，
日出有曜[①]。	太阳出来闪光耀。
岂不尔思？	难道我不想你吗？
中心是悼。	想你想得我哀伤。

---

① 有曜：在太阳的照耀下。

Songs Collected in Kuai, Modern Henan

The Last Lord of Kuai[1]

You seek amusement in official dress;
You hold your court in sacrificial gown.
How can we not think of you in distress?
O how can our heavy heart not sink down?

You find amusement in your lamb's fur dress;
In your fox's fur at court you appear.
How can we not think of you in distress?
O how can our heart not feel sad and drear?

You appear in your greasy dress
Which glistens in the sun.
How can we not think of you in distress?
We are heart-broken at the wrong you've done.

---

[1] The lamb's fur was used for official dress, but the lord of Kuai wore it while seeking amusement; the fox's fur was used for sacrificial dress, but the lord wore it at court. This showed that the lord neglected state affairs and that was the reason why the State of Kuai was extinguished by the State of Zheng in 769 B. C.

素　冠

庶①见素冠兮，　　　　　　　有幸再看见戴白帽的人啊，
棘②人栾栾③兮。　　　　　　见他又黑又瘦弱嶙峋啊。
劳心慱慱④兮。　　　　　　　心中悲痛啊。

庶见素衣兮，　　　　　　　　有幸再看见穿白衣的人啊，
我心伤悲兮。　　　　　　　　我的心中悲伤痛啊。
聊与子同归兮。　　　　　　　愿与你同归去啊。

庶见素韠⑤兮，　　　　　　　有幸再看见穿白裙的人啊，
我心蕴结兮。　　　　　　　　我的心中长郁闷啊。
聊与子如一兮。　　　　　　　誓愿与你同患难啊。

隰有苌楚⑥

隰有苌楚，　　　　　　　　　洼地长羊桃，
猗傩⑦其枝。　　　　　　　　枝叶多妖娆。

---

① 庶：幸，希望。
② 棘：即"瘠"，瘦弱。
③ 栾栾：瘦瘠的样子。
④ 慱慱：忧伤的样子。
⑤ 韠（bì）：蔽膝，裙。
⑥ 苌（cháng）楚：羊桃，猕猴桃。
⑦ 猗傩：枝叶柔弱，花实附枝，随风而舞的样子。

The Mourning Wife[1]

The deceased's white cap seen,
His worn-out face so lean,
I feel a sorrow keen.

Seeing my lord's white dress,
I become comfortless;
I would share his distress.

I see his white cover-knee,
Sorrow is knotted on me,
One with him I would be!

The Unconscious Tree[2]

In lowland grows the cherry
With branches swaying in high glee.

---

[1] It was said that mourners should wear white cap, white dress and white cover-knee since then.
[2] The speaker, groaning under the oppression of the government, wished he were an unconscious tree.

夭^①之沃沃^②,　　　　　　　细嫩又美好,
乐^③子^④之无知!　　　　　　羡你无知无烦恼!

隰有苌楚,　　　　　　　　　洼地长羊桃,
猗傩其华。　　　　　　　　　花朵多俊俏。
夭之沃沃,　　　　　　　　　细嫩又美好,
乐子之无家!　　　　　　　　羡你无家真逍遥!

隰有苌楚,　　　　　　　　　洼地长羊桃,
猗傩其实。　　　　　　　　　果实多美妙。
夭之沃沃,　　　　　　　　　细嫩又美好,
乐子之无室!　　　　　　　　羡你无家无妻小!

① 夭:草木初生嫩美的样子。
② 沃沃:光泽润滑的样子。
③ 乐:喜爱,羡慕。
④ 子:指苌楚。

Why do you look so merry?
I envy you, unconscious tree.

In lowland grows the cherry
With flowers blooming in the breeze.
Why do you look so merry?
I envy you quite at your ease.

In lowland grows the cherry
With fruit overloading the tree.
Why do you look so merry?
I envy you from cares so free.

匪 风

匪风发兮，　　　　　　　　那风儿吹动啊，
匪车偈①兮。　　　　　　　那车子开得快啊，
顾瞻周道，　　　　　　　　回头看看那大道，
中心怛②兮。　　　　　　　心中多么忧伤啊。

匪风飘兮，　　　　　　　　那风儿飘动啊，
匪车嘌③兮。　　　　　　　那车子摇动啊。
顾瞻周道，　　　　　　　　回头看看那大道，
中心吊兮。　　　　　　　　心中多么悽惶啊。

谁能亨④鱼？　　　　　　　谁能够烹煮鲜鱼？
溉⑤之釜鬵⑥。　　　　　　把锅儿洗干净。
谁将西归？　　　　　　　　谁要将向西边去？
怀之好音。　　　　　　　　请他报个平安回家乡。

① 偈（jié）：疾驰的样子。
② 怛（dá）：悲伤。
③ 嘌（piào）：飘摇不定。
④ 亨：即"烹"，煮。
⑤ 溉（gài）：洗。
⑥ 鬵（xín）：大锅。

Nostalgia[1]

The wind blows a strong blast;
The carriage's running fast.
I look to homeward, way.
Who can my grief allay?

The whirlwind blows a blast;
The cab runs wild and fast.
Looking to backward way,
Can I not pine away?

Who can boil fish?
I'll wash their boiler as they wish.
Who's going west?
Will he bring words at my request?

[1] This song spoke of King Ping's removal to the east as a result of the barbarian invasion in 769 B. C. when the State of Kuai, the poet's homeland, was extinguished by Duke Wu of Zheng (770—743 B. C.).

曹 风

蜉 蝣[①]

蜉蝣之羽,
衣裳楚楚。
心之忧矣,
于我归处!

蜉蝣的羽毛,
像鲜亮的衣裳。
我的心里忧伤,
究竟归处在何方!

蜉蝣之翼,
采采衣服。
心之忧矣,
于我归息!

蜉蝣的翅膀,
像明亮的衣服。
我的心里忧伤,
究竟归息在何方!

蜉蝣掘阅[②],
麻衣如雪。
心之忧矣,
于我归说[③]!

蜉蝣掘洞飞出,
洁白如雪麻衣服。
我的心里忧伤,
究竟归宿在何方!

---

① 蜉蝣:虫名,羽极薄而有光泽,多朝生暮死。
② 掘阅:即"掘穴",掘土而出。
③ 说:即"税",歇息。

Songs Collected in Cao, Modern Shandong

The Ephemera[1]

The ephemera's wings
Like morning robes are bright.
Grief to my heart it brings;
Where will it be at night?

The ephemera's wings
Like rainbow robes are bright.
Grief to my heart it brings;
Where will it rest by night?

The ephemera's hole
Like robe of hemp snow-white.
It brings grief to my soul:
Where may I go tonight?

---

[1] This was directed against Duke Zhao of Cao (reigned 661—651 B. C.)occupied with frivolous pleasures and oblivious of important matters. The small State of Cao was extinguished by Duke Jing of Song in 487 B. C.

候　人[1]

彼候人兮，	那个修路迎宾的小官啊，
何[2]戈与祋[3]。	扛着长戈和长棍。
彼其之子，	他们那些人啊，
三百赤芾[4]。	三百多人穿着大红蔽膝的人。
维鹈[5]在梁，	只是鹈鸟在鱼梁上，
不濡其翼。	没有打湿它的翅膀。
彼其之子，	他们那些人啊，
不称其服。	不配他们的好衣裳。
维鹈在梁，	只是鹈鸟在鱼梁上，
不濡其咮[6]。	没有沾湿它的嘴巴。
彼其之子，	他们那些人啊，
不遂其媾[7]。	不配他们的高官厚禄。
荟兮蔚兮[8]，	云雾弥漫啊，
南山朝隮[9]。	南山早上升彩虹。

① 候人：修路迎宾的官。
② 何：即"荷"，扛着。
③ 祋（duì）：殳，一种兵器。
④ 赤芾（fú）：红蔽膝，大夫朝服的一部分。
⑤ 鹈：水鸟名。
⑥ 咮（zhòu）：鸟嘴。
⑦ 媾：厚禄。
⑧ 荟蔚：云雾弥漫的样子。
⑨ 朝隮（jī）：彩虹。

Poor Attendants[①]

Holding halberds and spears,
The attendants escort
The rich three hundred peers,
Wearing red cover-knee in court.

The pelicans catch fish
Without wetting their wings;
The peers have what they wish,
But they're unworthy things.

The pelicans catch fish
Without wetting their beak;
The peers do what they wish,
Unworthy of favor they seek.

At sunrise on south hill
The attendants still wait;

[①] This was directed against Duke Gong of Cao who had three hundred worthless peers but only one hundred diligent attennndants in his court and who was impolite to Duke Wen of Jin in 641 B. C.

婉兮娈兮，　　　　　　　　柔婉啊娇美啊，
季女斯饥。　　　　　　　　幼小的女儿忍着饥饿。

鸤鸠①

鸤鸠在桑，　　　　　　　　布谷鸟筑巢桑树间，
其子七兮。　　　　　　　　它的儿子有七个啊。
淑人君子，　　　　　　　　善良的君子人啊，
其仪一兮。　　　　　　　　他的仪容是一样啊。
其仪一兮，　　　　　　　　他的仪容是一样啊，
心如结兮。　　　　　　　　忠心耿耿如石坚啊。

鸤鸠在桑，　　　　　　　　布谷鸟筑巢桑树间，
其子在梅。　　　　　　　　它的儿子在梅树上。
淑人君子，　　　　　　　　善良的君子人啊，
其带伊丝。　　　　　　　　他的带子镶边用白丝。
其带伊丝，　　　　　　　　他的带子镶边用白丝，
其弁②伊骐③。　　　　　　玉饰皮帽镶青丝。

鸤鸠在桑，　　　　　　　　布谷鸟筑巢桑树间，
其子在棘。　　　　　　　　它的儿子在酸枣树上。
淑人君子，　　　　　　　　善良的君子人啊，
其仪不忒。　　　　　　　　他的威仪不改变。

---

① 鸤鸠（shī jiū）：布谷鸟。
② 弁：帽子。
③ 伊骐：青黑色的马，指青黑色。

Their hungry daughters feel ill,
Weeping their bitter fate.

An Ideal Ruler[1]

The cuckoo in the mulberries
Breeds seven fledglings with ease.
An ideal ruler should take care
To deal with all men fair and square.
If he treats all men fair and square,
He would be good beyond compare.

The cuckoo in the mulberries
Breeds fledglings in mume trees.
An ideal ruler should be fair and bright,
His girdle hemmed with silk white.
If he's as bright as silken hems,
He'd be adorned with jade and gems.

The cuckoo in the mulberries
Breeds fledglings in the jujube trees.
An ideal ruler should be polite;
Whatever he does should be right.

---

[1] An ideal ruler was celebrated by way of contrast with the rulers of the State of Cao.

其仪不忒，　　　　　　他的威仪不改变，
正①是四国。　　　　　　可以做四国的榜样。

鸤鸠在桑，　　　　　　布谷鸟筑巢桑树间，
其子在榛。　　　　　　它的儿子在榛树上。
淑人君子，　　　　　　善良的君子人啊，
正是国人。　　　　　　是国人的好榜样。
正是国人，　　　　　　是国人的好榜样，
胡不万年！　　　　　　何不祈祝他寿无疆！

下　泉

冽②彼下泉，　　　　　　冰冷的泉水向下流，
浸彼苞稂③。　　　　　　淹那丛生的莠草根。
忾④我寤叹，　　　　　　我醒来只有叹息，
念彼周京。　　　　　　想念那周朝的京城。

冽彼下泉，　　　　　　冰冷的泉水向下流，
浸彼苞萧。　　　　　　浸那丛生的蒿草根。
忾我寤叹，　　　　　　我醒来只有叹息，
念彼京周。　　　　　　想念那周朝的京城。

① 正：法则，榜样。
② 冽：寒冷。
③ 稂（láng）：狗尾草。
④ 忾（xì）：叹息。

If he is right as magistrate,
He'd be a model for the state.

The cuckoo in the mulberries
Breeds fledglings in the hazel trees.
Ruler should be a good magistrate
To help the people of the state.
If he helps people to right the wrong,
May he live ten thousand years loiag!

The Canal[①]

The bushy grass drowned by
Cold water flowing down,
When I awake, I sigh
For our capital town.

The southernwood drowned by
Cold water flowing down,
When I awake, I sigh
For our municipal town.

[①] The bushy grass and plants drowned in cold water might allude to the small State of Cao drowned in misery which made the writer think of the capital of Zhou and of its prosperity.

冽彼下泉，　　　　　　　　冰冷的泉水向下流，
浸彼苞蓍①。　　　　　　　淹那丛生的蓍草根。
忾我寤叹，　　　　　　　　我醒来只有叹息，
念彼京师。　　　　　　　　想念那周朝的京城。

芃芃②黍苗，　　　　　　　蓬蓬勃勃的黍苗，
阴雨膏③之。　　　　　　　雨水来润泽它们。
四国④有王⑤，　　　　　　四方诸侯上朝来，
郇伯⑥劳之。　　　　　　　郇伯一一来慰劳。

① 蓍：草名，古人作来占筮。
② 芃芃：草木茂盛的样子。
③ 膏：滋润。
④ 四国：四方诸侯之国。
⑤ 有王：有周天子。
⑥ 郇（xún）伯：郇国的国君。

The bushy plants drowned by
Cold water flowing down,
When I awake, I sigh
For our old royal town,

Where millet grew in spring,
Enriched by happy rain;
The state ruled by the wise king,
The toilers had their grain.

豳 风

七 月

七月流火①，	七月里火星偏向西，
九月授衣。	九月里女工缝衣裳。
一之日②觱发③，	十一月里起寒风，
二之日栗烈④。	十二月里风刺骨。
无衣无褐⑤，	没有长袍和短袄，
何以卒岁？	怎么才能过冬天？
三之日于耜⑥，	正月里修理家具，
四之日举趾⑦。	二月里下地春耕。
同我妇子，	叫我妻子和儿女，
馌⑧彼南亩，	把饭送到田地头，
田畯⑨至喜。	田官看了心喜欢。
七月流火，	七月里火星偏向西，
九月授衣。	九月里官家发寒衣。

---

① 流火：火星向西下行。
② 一之日：周历的正月，夏历的十一月。二之日、三之日以此类推。
③ 觱发（bì bō）：寒风吹动的声音。
④ 栗烈：凛烈。
⑤ 褐：粗布衣服。
⑥ 耜：耒耜，犁的一种。
⑦ 举趾：举足下田耕地。
⑧ 馌（yè）：给耕地的人送饭到地头。
⑨ 田畯（jùn）：田官，监督奴隶们劳动的人。

Songs Collected in Bin, Modern Shaanxi

Life of Peasants[①]

In seventh moon Fire Star west goes;
In ninth to make dress we are told.
In eleventh moon the wind blows;
In twelfth the weather is cold.
We have no warm garments to wear.
How can we get through the year?
In the first moon we mend our plough with care;
In the second our way afield we steer.
Our wives and children take the food
To southern fields; the overseer says, "Good!"

In seventh moon Fire Star west goes;
In ninth we make dress all day long.

---

① This was a description of the life of the peasants in Bin, where the first settlers of the House of Zhou dwelt for nearly five centuries from 1796 to 1325 B. C.

春日载阳①，	春天太阳暖洋洋，
有鸣仓庚②。	黄莺枝头声声啼。
女执懿筐③，	姑娘提着深竹筐，
遵④彼微行⑤，	沿着小路向前走，
爰求柔桑。	采呀采呀采嫩桑。
春日迟迟⑥，	春天日子渐渐长，
采蘩祁祁⑦。	采摘白蒿忙又忙。
女心伤悲，	姑娘心里暗悲伤，
殆⑧及⑨公子同归⑩。	怕与公子一起回。
七月流火，	七月里火星偏向西，
八月萑苇⑪。	八月里割苇好收藏。
蚕月⑫条桑⑬，	三月里剪枝条桑，
取彼斧斨⑭。	拿起斧子去砍伐。
以伐远扬⑮，	高枝长条砍干净，
猗彼女桑。	攀着短枝摘嫩桑。

① 载阳：开始暖和。
② 仓庚：黄鹂。
③ 懿筐：深筐。
④ 遵：沿着。
⑤ 微行：小路。
⑥ 迟迟：春日渐长的样子。
⑦ 祁祁：采蘩的人很多的样子。
⑧ 殆：怕。
⑨ 及：与。
⑩ 同归：强行带去作妾婢。
⑪ 萑（huán）苇：芦苇。
⑫ 蚕月：夏历三月是养蚕之月，所以称三月为蚕月。
⑬ 条桑：修剪桑枝。
⑭ 斨（qiāng）：柄孔方的斧。
⑮ 远扬：长得又长又高的桑枝。

By and by warm spring grows
And golden orioles sing their song.
The lasses take their baskets deep
And go along the small pathways
To gather tender mulberry leaves in heap.
When lengthen vernal days,
They pile in heaps the southernwood.
They are in gloomy mood.
For they will say adieu to maidenhood.

In seventh moon Fire Star west goes;
In eighth we gather rush and reed.
In silkworm month with axe's blow
We cut mulberry sprigs with speed.
We lop off branches long and high
And bring young tender leaves in.

七月鸣䴗①，	七月里伯劳树上叫，
八月载绩②。	八月里纺麻又织布。
载玄载黄，	染成黑色染成黄色，
我朱孔阳③，	我染成红色最漂亮，
为公子裳。	为那公子做件衣裳。
四月秀④葽⑤，	四月里远志结子，
五月鸣蜩。	五月里蝉鸣不止。
八月其获，	八月里庄稼收割，
十月陨萚⑥。	十月里落叶飘飞。
一之日于貉，	十一月上山打貉。
取彼狐狸，	取那狐狸剥下皮，
为公子裘。	做件皮袄给公子。
二之日其同，	十二月里大聚会，
载缵⑦武功⑧。	继续打猎练武功。
言私其豵⑨，	小猪自己留下来，
献豜⑩于公。	大猪送到公府去。
五月斯螽⑪动股，	五月里斯螽弹动腿，
六月莎鸡⑫振羽。	六月里蝈蝈抖翅膀。

① 䴗(jú)：鸟名，又叫伯劳。
② 绩：织麻。
③ 孔阳：很鲜亮。
④ 秀：植物不开花而结实。
⑤ 葽(yāo)：草名，远志。
⑥ 萚(tuò)：草木落下的枝叶皮等。
⑦ 缵：继续。
⑧ 武功：武事，打猎。
⑨ 豵(zōng)：小野猪。
⑩ 豜(jiān)：大野猪。
⑪ 斯螽：蚱蜢。
⑫ 莎(suō)鸡：虫名，纺织娘。

In seventh moon we hear shrikes cry;
In eighth moon we begin to spin.
We use a bright red dye
And a dark yellow one
To color robes of our lord's son.

In fourth moon grass begins to seed;
In fifth cicadas cry.
In eighth moon to reap we proceed;
In tenth down eome leaves dry.
In eleventh moon we go in chase
For wild cats and foxes fleet
To make furs for the sons of noble race.

In the twelfth moon we meet
And manoeuvre with lance and sword.
We keep the smaller boars for our reward
And offer larger ones o'er to our lord.
In fifth moon locusts move their legs;
In sixth the spinner shakes its wings.
In seventh the cricket lays its eggs;
In eighth under the eaves it sings.

七月在野,	七月蟋蟀在田野,
八月在宇,	八月屋檐底下唱,
九月在户,	九月跳进房门来,
十月蟋蟀入我床下。	十月在我床下藏。
穹窒①熏鼠,	塞住漏洞熏老鼠,
塞向②墐③户。	堵上北窗封好门。
嗟我妇子,	感叹我的妻子和儿女,
曰为改岁④,	眼看就要过年了,
入此室处。	住进这屋里避风寒。
六月食郁及薁⑤,	六月吃李子和葡萄,
七月亨葵及菽。	七月煮葵苗烧豆汤。
八月剥枣,	八月打下大红枣,
十月获稻。	十月收割稻米香。
为此春酒,	用来酿春酒,
以介⑥眉寿⑦。	喝来祝长寿。
七月食瓜,	七月吃瓜果,
八月断⑧壶⑨,	八月摘葫芦,
九月叔苴。	九月拣芝麻。
采荼薪樗,	采苦菜砍些柴,
食⑩我农夫。	养活我们农夫们。

① 穹窒(zhì): 室中洞隙加以堵塞。
② 向: 北窗。
③ 墐(jǐn): 用泥土涂抹。
④ 改岁: 过年。
⑤ 薁(yù): 野葡萄。
⑥ 介: 祈求。
⑦ 眉寿: 高寿的人眉毛长,所以称高寿的人为眉寿。
⑧ 断: 摘下。
⑨ 壶: 葫芦。
⑩ 食(sì): 养活。

In ninth it moves indoors when chilled;
In tenth it enters under the bed.
We clear the corners, chinks are filled,
We smoke the house and rats run in dread.
We plaster northern window and door
And tell our wives and lad and lass;
The old year' will soon be no more.
Let's dwell inside, alas!

In sixth moon we've wild plums and grapes to eat;
In seventh we cook beans and mallows nice.
In eighth moon down the dates we beat;
In tenth we reap the rice
And brew the vernal wine,
A cordial for the oldest-grown.
In seventh moon we eat melon fine;
In eighth moon the gourds are cut down.
In ninth we gather the hemp-seed;
Of fetid tree we make firewood;
We gather lettuce to feed
Our husbandmen as food.

九月筑场①圃，　　　　　　　九月修好打谷场，
十月纳禾稼。　　　　　　　　十月庄稼要进仓。
黍稷重穋②，　　　　　　　　谷子高粱早晚熟，
禾麻菽麦。　　　　　　　　　粟麻豆麦一起藏。
嗟我农夫！　　　　　　　　　嗟叹我们农夫！
我稼既同③，　　　　　　　　庄稼刚刚收完，
上入执宫功：　　　　　　　　还要服役修官房：
昼尔于茅，　　　　　　　　　白天割来茅草，
宵尔索绹④，　　　　　　　　晚上搓好绳子，
亟其乘屋，　　　　　　　　　急忙去修屋顶，
其始播百谷。　　　　　　　　开春又要种谷。

二之日凿冰冲冲，　　　　　　十二月凿冰冲冲响，
三之日纳于凌阴⑤。　　　　　正月里把冰藏冰窖。
四之日其蚤⑥，　　　　　　　二月里起早来祭祀，
献羔祭韭。　　　　　　　　　献上韭菜和羔羊。
九月肃霜，　　　　　　　　　九月里天高气爽，
十月涤场⑦。　　　　　　　　十月里清扫打谷场。
朋酒斯飨，　　　　　　　　　两壶美酒可飨，
曰杀羔羊，　　　　　　　　　再杀羔羊佐酒。
跻⑧彼公堂，　　　　　　　　登上台阶进公堂，

① 场：打谷场。
② 重穋（lù）：庄稼后熟叫重，先熟叫穋。
③ 同：收齐集中。
④ 绹（táo）：绳子。
⑤ 凌阴：冰窖。
⑥ 蚤：早晨。
⑦ 涤场：一年农事完毕，打扫场圃。
⑧ 跻：登上。

In ninth moon we repair the threshing-floor;
In tenth we bring in harvest clean;
The millet sown early and late are put in store,
And wheat and hemp, paddy and bean.
There is no rest for husbandmen:
Once harvesting is done, alas!
We're sent to work in lord's house then.
By day for thatch we gather reed and grass;
At night we twist them into ropes,
Then hurry to mend the roofs again,
For we should not abandon the hopes
Of sowing in time our fields with grain.

In the twelfth moon we hew out ice;
In the first moon we store it deep.
In the second we offer early sacrifice
Of garlic, lamb and sheep.
In ninth moon frosty is the weather;
In tenth we sweep and clear the threshing-floor.
We drink two bottles of wine together
And kill a lamb before the door.

称①彼兕觥②,　　　　　　　　　高高举起牛角杯,
万寿无疆!　　　　　　　　　　同声高唱寿无疆!

鸱鸮③

鸱鸮鸱鸮,　　　　　　　　　　猫头鹰啊猫头鹰,
既取我子,　　　　　　　　　　你已经抓走我的小鸟,
无毁我室。　　　　　　　　　　就不是要毁我的家了。
恩斯勤斯,　　　　　　　　　　辛勤养护我的宝小鸟,
鬻④子之闵⑤斯!　　　　　　　为了养它我又累又乏!
迨天之未阴雨,　　　　　　　　等着天晴没有阴雨,
彻彼桑土,　　　　　　　　　　剥下桑树根上的皮,
绸缪⑥牖户⑦。　　　　　　　　修补窗子和门户。
今女下民,　　　　　　　　　　现在你们下面的人,
或敢侮予!　　　　　　　　　　还有谁敢来欺侮!

予手拮据⑧,　　　　　　　　　我的手已经疲劳,
予所捋荼,　　　　　　　　　　我还要采茅草,
予所蓄租⑨。　　　　　　　　　我还要贮存草。

① 称: 举杯。
② 兕觥 (sì): 兕牛角制成的酒器。
③ 鸱鸮 (chī xiāo): 猫头鹰。
④ 鬻 (yù): 养育。
⑤ 闵: 怜恤, 疾病。
⑥ 绸缪: 缠缚, 结扎。
⑦ 牖户: 指鸟窝。
⑧ 拮据: 劳累过度, 脚爪麻木。
⑨ 租: 干茅草。

Then we go up to the hall where
We raise our buffalo-horn cup
And wish our lord to live fore'er.

A Mother Bird[1]

Owl, owl, you've
Taken my young ones away.
Do not destroy my nest!
With love and pain I toiled all day
To hatch them without rest.
Before it is going to rain,
I gather roots of mulberry
And mend my nest with might and main
Lest others bully me.

My claws feel sore
From gathering reeds without rest;
I put them up in store
Until my beak feels pain to mend my nest.

---

[1] This was the first fable in Chinese poetry.

予口卒瘏①,　　　　　　　　我的嘴巴累坏了,
曰予未有室家!　　　　　　我的窝还没有修好!

予羽谯谯②,　　　　　　　我的羽毛已经稀少,
予尾翛翛③。　　　　　　　我的尾巴已经枯焦。
予室翘翘④,　　　　　　　我的窝还在晃摇,
风雨所漂摇,　　　　　　　风吹雨打多飘摇,
予维音哓哓⑤!　　　　　　我只有大声喊叫。

东　山

我徂⑥东山,　　　　　　　我远征到东山,
慆慆⑦不归。　　　　　　　长久不能回来。
我来自东,　　　　　　　　我从东方回来,
零雨⑧其濛。　　　　　　　小雨迷蒙落下来。
我东曰归,　　　　　　　　我从东方回来,
我心西悲。　　　　　　　　想到西方心悲伤。
制彼裳衣⑨,　　　　　　　缝制家常的衣裳,
勿士行枚⑩。　　　　　　　再不用行军衔枚。

---

① 卒瘏（tú）：劳累致病。
② 谯谯：羽毛稀疏的样子。
③ 翛翛：羽毛枯焦的样子。
④ 翘翘：摇晃，危险的样子。
⑤ 哓哓（xiāo xiāo）：惊恐的叫声。
⑥ 徂：往。
⑦ 慆慆（tāo tāo）：时间长久。
⑧ 零雨：下得又慢又细的小雨。
⑨ 裳衣：普通人所着的服装。
⑩ 行枚：即"衔枚",为了行军时不发出声音。

Sparse is my feather
And torn my tail
My nest is tossed in stormy weather;
I cry and wail to no avail.

Coming Back From the Eastern Hills[①]

To east hills sent away,
Long did I there remain.
Now on my westward way,
There falls a drizzling rain.
Knowing I'll be back from the east,
My heart yearns for the west.
Fighting no more at least,
I'll wear a farmer's vest.

[①] The Duke of Zhou put down a rebellion in the east after 1125 B. C.

蜎蜎①者蠋②,　　　　　　　蠕动的毛毛虫,
烝③在桑野。　　　　　　　趴在那桑树上。
敦④彼独宿,　　　　　　　蜷缩的人独自睡,
亦在车下。　　　　　　　独自睡在战车下。

我徂东山,　　　　　　　我远征到东山,
慆慆不归。　　　　　　　长久不能回来。
我来自东,　　　　　　　我从东方回来,
零雨其濛。　　　　　　　小雨迷蒙落下来。
果臝⑤之实,　　　　　　　瓜蒌结的子儿大,
亦施于宇。　　　　　　　子儿结在屋檐下。
伊威⑥在室,　　　　　　　土鳖儿在屋里爬,
蠨蛸⑦在户。　　　　　　　蜘蛛结网在门上。
町疃⑧鹿场,　　　　　　　野鹿在场上回旋,
熠燿⑨宵行⑩。　　　　　　萤火虫儿光闪闪。
不可畏也?　　　　　　　家园荒凉不可怕?
伊可怀也?　　　　　　　它是多么让人牵挂?

我徂东山,　　　　　　　我远征到东山,
慆慆不归。　　　　　　　长久不能回来。

① 蜎蜎(yuān yuān):蠕动的样子。
② 蠋:毛虫。
③ 烝:久,留,多。
④ 敦:蜷曲成一团。
⑤ 果臝(luǒ):植物名,瓜蒌。
⑥ 伊威:虫名,土鳖。
⑦ 蠨蛸(xiāo shāo):蜘蛛。
⑧ 町疃(tǐng tuǎn):野外。
⑨ 熠燿:萤光发光的样子。
⑩ 宵行:萤火虫。

Curled up as silkworm crept
On the mtilberry tree,
Beneath my cart alone I slept.
O how it saddened me!

To east hills sent away,
Long did I there remain.
Now on my westward way,
There falls a drizzling rain.
The vide of gourd may clamber
The wall and eave all o'er;
I may find woodlice in my chamber
And cobwebs across the door;
I may see in paddock deer-track
And glow-worms' fitful light.
Still I long to be back
To see such sorry sight.

To east hills sent away,
Long did I there remain.

我来自东,	我从东方回来,
零雨其濛。	小雨迷蒙落下来。
鹳①鸣于垤②,	老鹳在墩上不停叫,
妇叹于室。	我妻在屋里不停叹。
洒扫穹室,	打扫屋子塞鼠洞,
我征聿至③。	行人离家不远了。
有敦瓜苦,	有人葫芦团又团,
烝在栗薪。	撂在柴堆没有管。
自我不见,	从我不见这些事,
于今三年。	直到今天已三年。
我徂东山,	我远征到东山,
慆慆不归。	长久不能回来。
我来自东,	我从东方回来,
零雨其濛。	小雨迷蒙落下来。
仓庚于飞,	记得那天黄鹂飞,
熠耀其羽。	羽毛闪闪映着光。
之子于归,	这个姑娘要出嫁,
皇驳④其马。	马儿有红也有黄。
亲结其缡⑤,	娘为女儿结佩巾,
九十其仪⑥。	多种仪式真堂皇。

① 鹳:鸟名,似鹤。
② 垤(dié):土堆。
③ 聿至:即将到。
④ 驳:红白相杂。
⑤ 缡(lí):古代妇女的佩巾,出嫁时母亲为女儿结戴佩巾。
⑥ 仪:仪式。

Now on my westward way,
There falls a drizzling rain.
The cranes on ant-hill cry;
My wife in cottage room
May sprinkle, sweep and sigh
For my returning home.
The gourd may still hang high
Beside the chestnut tree.
O three years have gone by
Since last she was with me.

To east hills sent away,
long did I there remain.
Now on my westward way,
There falls a drizzling rain.
The oriole takes flight
with glinting wings outspread.
I remember on horse bright
My bride came to be wed.
Her sash by her mother tied,
She should observe the rite.

其新孔嘉,　　　　　　　　想想新娘真是美,
其旧如之何?　　　　　　　久别重逢会怎样?

破 斧

既破我斧,　　　　　　　　我的斧子破了,
又缺我斨①。　　　　　　　我的斨子缺口。
周公东征,　　　　　　　　周公向东讨伐,
四国②是皇③。　　　　　　四国得到安匡。
哀我人斯,　　　　　　　　我们战士多辛劳啊,
亦孔之将。　　　　　　　　立下的功劳真不少。

既破我斧,　　　　　　　　我的斧子破了,
又缺我锜④。　　　　　　　我的凿子缺口。
周公东征,　　　　　　　　周公向东讨伐,
四国是吪⑤。　　　　　　　四国得到教化。
哀我人斯,　　　　　　　　我们战士多辛劳啊,
亦孔之嘉。　　　　　　　　立下的功劳得好评。

既破我斧,　　　　　　　　我的斧子破了,
又缺我銶⑥。　　　　　　　我的铁锹缺口。
周公东征,　　　　　　　　周公向东讨伐,

---

① 斨(qiāng):斧柄方孔的叫斨。
② 四国:四方之国。
③ 皇:匡正。
④ 锜(qí):凿子。
⑤ 吪(é):教化。
⑥ 銶(qiú):铁锹。

Happy was I to meet my bride;
How happy when my wife's in sight!

With Broken Axe[1]

With broken axe in hand
And hatchet, our poor mates
Follow our duke from eastern land;
We've conquered the four States.
Alas! Those who are not strong
Cannot come along.

With broken axe in hand
And chisel, our poor mates
Follow our duke from eastern land;
We've controlled the four States.
Alas! Those who do not survive!
Lucky those still alive.

With broken axe in hand
And halberd, our poor mates
Follow our duke from eastern land

---

[1] In 1125 B. C. the Duke of Zhou undertook an expedition against the four eastern states ruled by his own brothers Guan and Cai and Yah and the son of the last king of Shang. The battles were so fierce that many axes and hatchets were broken, and it took him three years to put down the rebellion.

四国是道①。	四国得到安定。
哀我人斯，	我们战士多辛劳啊，
亦孔之休。	立下的功劳值得夸。

伐 柯

伐柯如何？	怎么去砍那斧柄？
匪斧不克，	没有斧子怎能行。
取妻如何？	怎么去娶那妻子？
匪媒不得。	没有媒人怎能行。
伐柯伐柯，	砍斧柄啊砍斧柄，
其则不远。	它的法则在近旁。
我觏之子，	我遇见这个姑娘，
笾②豆③有践④。	把餐具排列成行。

九 罭⑤

九罭之鱼，	捕小鱼的细网，
鳟鲂。	捉住了鳟与鲂。
我觏之子，	我看见这个人，
衮衣⑥绣裳。	穿着龙袍绣裳。

① 道：安定。
② 笾（biān）：盛果品的竹器。
③ 豆：盛肉的木器。
④ 践：行列。
⑤ 九罭（yù）：捕小鱼的细网。
⑥ 衮衣：绣着龙的礼服。

We've ruled o'er the four States.
Alas! Those who are dead!
Lucky, let's go ahead.

An Axe-handle[①]

Do you know how to make
An axe-handle? With an axe keen.
Do you know how to take
A wife? Just ask a go-between.

When a handle is hewed,
The pattern should not be far.
When a maiden is wooed,
See how many betrothal gifts there are.

The Duke's Return[②]

In a nine-bagged net
There are breams and red-eyes.
See ducal coronet
And gown on which the broidered dragon flies.

---

① It was said that this song was sung by a bridegroom to his unmarried friends. That was the reason why a go-between was called a handlemaker in China.
② The people of the eastern states expressed their admiration of the Duke of Zhou and sorrow at his return to the capital in 1122 B. C..

鸿飞遵渚,	大雁沿着沙滩飞,
公归无所?	公爷难道没归处?
于女信①处。	暂在这里住两宿。
鸿飞遵陆,	大雁沿着大陆飞,
公归不复,	公爷离去不再回。
于女信宿。	请在这里住一会儿。
是以有衮衣兮!	把龙袍留在这里啊!
无以我公归兮!	别让公爷回去啊!
无使我心悲兮!	别再让我悲伤啊!

狼 跋②

狼跋其胡,	狼向前进踩颔下肉,
载疐③其尾。	向后退又踩大尾巴。
公孙硕肤④,	公孙心宽又体胖,
赤舄⑤几几⑥。	饰金鞋头多漂亮。

狼疐其尾,	狼后退踩大尾巴,
载跋其胡。	向前进踩颔下肉。
公孙硕肤,	公孙心宽又体胖,
德音不瑕。	声名美誉传远方。

---

① 信: 住两晚。
② 跋: 兽颔下的垂肉。
③ 疐(zhì): 踩。
④ 硕肤: 心宽体胖。
⑤ 赤舄(xì): 金属的鞋头饰物。
⑥ 几几: 盛装的样子。

Along the shore the swan's in flight.
Where will our duke alight?
He stops with us only tonight.
The swan's in flight along the track.
Our duke, once gone, will not come back.
His soldiers pass the night in bivouac.
Let's keep his broidered gown.
May he not leave our town
Lest in regret our heart will drown!

Like an Old Wolf[1]

The duke can't go ahead
Nor at his ease retreat.
He's good to put on slippers red
And leave the regent's seat.

The duke cannot retreat
Nor with ease forward go.
He's good to leave his seat
And keep his fame aglow.

---

[1] The Duke of Zhou was regent, in 1115 B. C., but he could neither advance nor retreat, for if he should advance, the rumor would spread that he would seize the throne; if he should retreat, the young king would be dethroned. He was like an old wolf Which would be hindered by its dewlap in advancing and would tread on its own tail in retreating. The Duke left the regent's seat and restored King Cheng to the throne in 1109 B. C.